PRAISE FOR *IN MY MOTHER'S HOUSE*
BY MARGARET MCMULLAN

"Haunting." *–Lifetime Magazine*

"The two narrative threads blend into one
harmonious story." *–Entertainment Weekly*

"It is the individual, private pain it caused that is skillfully
given voice here by Margaret McMullan." *–Boston Globe*

AFTERMATH LOUNGE

by Margaret McMullan

CALYPSO EDITIONS

CALYPSO EDITIONS
www. CalypsoEditions.org

By unearthing literary gems from previous generations, translating foreign writers into English with integrity, and providing a space for talented new voices, Calypso Editions is committed to publishing books that will endure in both content and form. Our only criterion is excellence.

ISBN: 978-0-9887903-6-0

Cover photo courtesy of Alan Huffman

First printing, March 2015
Printed in the United States

For my mother-in-law, Mary Jane O'Connor

CONTENTS

HURRICANE SEASON

Baby Charlie was already there in the kitchen squalling when a woman from some office in Hancock County called to say they had Donna's will and it looked like it had been Donna's wish for Norma to become legal guardian. As Charlie arched his back and howled on a blanket on the floor, Norma shouted into the phone, "Are you sure?" and opened up another beer.

Norma went drunk to the funeral with her husband, Sam, and baby Charlie. In her blur, she held out hope that she would meet up with some of Donna's people. They would know what to do with the child. But the only other people there were the priest and the few people Donna had gone out drinking with that night, the night of the wreck. At the grave site, they all stood without moving as they watched a man in a truck lower a cable that held the pine box in which Donna lay. Norma could feel the wet grass through her shoes as she watched. The casket bumped the side of the hole as it was lowered, and for one long instant, it hung on the lip. Clumps of soggy red dirt rolled down the side into the hole. Some people left, but Norma stayed. She had heard that sometimes a crooked undertaker would dump a body out of the casket then resell the casket. Her white heels sank deep into the ground, and she stayed until the man with the backhoe had shoved the last pile of red clay on Donna.

Afterwards, they ended up at somebody's place near a fish store, and as they all kicked around the oyster shells in the driveway, they talked about how someone must have screwed up the brakes on Donna's car when she had them fixed the week before. Surely someone was to blame for this *devastation*.

The petunias all around the driveway were sticky and spent and whatever was left of anything was ghost gray. Sam sat on the porch swing smoking, watching Norma, and rocking Charlie who was wearing the same Cheeto-colored t-shirt he'd been wearing the night his mother died. Every now and then Charlie knocked against the cast on Sam's leg. Neither one of them seemed to mind. Sam had broken his leg putting the roof on a new video store two weeks before. Donna had left Charlie with Norma that last night she went out, had even kissed Norma goodbye, her lips moist from beer, and said, "Wish me luck," because she wanted to meet a man. As Norma drank and listened to the talk in the driveway, she settled back into what she already knew: she didn't want Donna dead and she didn't want Donna's six-month-old baby boy, Charlie.

That night in the bedroom, Norma sipped bourbon straight and tried singing her own version of "It's a Small World, After All," but she didn't know all the words, so she fixed on "Amazing Grace," a song she recalled her mother singing to her. Still, Charlie cried. Norma imagined he cried because he didn't have any words. She watched in amazement as he wailed, his lips growing plump, his dark little head turning red and hot, until at last he arched his back and thrust his face skyward in a final spasm of anger and sorrow.

"Holy hell," Sam said, looking in on them. He limped away, then closed the door to their bedroom, saying he'd sleep on the sofa.

"I know, I know sugar," Norma said to Charlie. "Maybe you and me can make a nice eggnog later on."

She knew Charlie would have no memory of his mother but she also knew his body remembered in ways that his mind could not. She did not know how she knew this, she just did.

Neither Sam nor Norma had ever had any children. It simply had not happened, and by the time they had reached their mid-forties and their second marriages, it was too late. Norma put her little finger in her glass of bourbon and touched Charlie's lips. The baby stopped crying at first only because he tasted something new, then he cried more because of the newness. Norma tried another finger of bourbon, and finally Charlie quieted down. Rocking him in her arms, Norma cried and drank, hating death and hating Sam for being the only thing she had left.

It rained all day the day after Donna's funeral. It was almost October and hurricane season wasn't over yet on the Mississippi Gulf Coast. For years, people in Gulfport were predicting a bigger one—bigger than Andrew, bigger even than Camille. There had been quite a few tropical depressions, a sure sign of bigger things to come. By the time Norma finished setting up the crib, she started a second six pack, and the rain came down in sheets.

"Maybe it's a blessing," she said, putting down the beer to rock Charlie with both hands. They had already gotten Charlie's things from Donna's place and the bags of clothes, diapers, and formula were all around them.

"Some way to get blessed," Sam said, scratching the skin around the top of his cast.

That night Charlie finally fell asleep, leaving Norma awake and alone, staring at her husband's back as he typed at his computer in the next room. Sam hadn't worked since he'd fallen off that roof. He had talked about getting a job at the new casino when his leg healed, but then he went and bought a computer at a yard sale and spent $450 to take an online computer class. At least they were both off the cocaine.

Norma went over and nuzzled up to Sam. She wanted to lose the feeling of being tired, to forget about Donna and death. She concentrated on Sam's shoulders and attempted to get back the feeling of being in love. She thought about that warm, rainy night, inside Sam's first car—the blue one. They had fogged up all the windows then, leaned back in their seats, and with his big toe, Sam drew a heart on the windshield, writing *I Love U* on the inside. Norma thought about this, trying to recall that feeling she had had then when she read the inside of Sam's heart.

"You're hanging on me, babe," Sam said, reading something on his screen then copying it down on his cast. The cast went all the way down to his toes, but Sam's notes only reached as far as his knee.

"I can keep on cleaning houses. I'll just bring Charlie with me the way Donna did. You find out anything more about that casino job?"

"Leave me be," Sam said. "Can't you see I'm in class?"

"We have another mouth to feed, you know."

Sam swirled around in his chair. There were dark rings under his eyes and he hadn't shaved. "Don't you think I know that? Would you leave me alone for one minute? I'm trying to do something here."

"OK, OK," Norma said, backing up.

Sam turned back to his computer. Norma stood in the doorway, staring at her husband's shoulders rounded like a woman's. The room he called his office smelled of coffee and unwashed bodies.

Norma got another beer. Ever since Sam had hooked himself up to the World Wide Web, he didn't look at TV and he didn't look at her. Norma wondered what they said to each other in their online chat rooms—her husband and these other people—women, most likely. She'd read about such things in the newspapers, heard about their stories on TV talk shows. Even Donna had warned her, and everyone knew that Donna had some Choctaw witch in her.

If she emailed someone about her life now, Norma thought about the mountain of dirty dishes and laundry that would fill her on-screen letters. Then there were the groceries and the water, electric and phone bills. And now there were the diapers and ointment and bottles of formula. There was and there was and there was, and these all filled whole days, weeks, and months that would make up the years and Norma wondered who would be interested in all this junk that made up her life. Changing into her nightgown, Norma wondered, momentarily, if she should start going back to church. Then she considered leaving Sam.

She lay in bed with the windows open, and even though she didn't mean to, Norma caught herself thinking back to the times she'd spent with her first husband, Catch. His fingertips smelled of shrimp shells and she had liked the tobacco taste of his mouth. But after she left, she had to put a restraining order on him, then he landed up in jail anyway for a handful of DUIs. He was a freckled, brown-haired man who did drink too much and who did hit her once or twice—it was true— but he was always trying to make Norma laugh.

Hot and tired, Norma got up out of bed. She had a taste in her mouth now for bourbon and Coke.

All along the waterfront people were closing up their houses, hammering fitted plywood over windows, and locking their shutters. Miss Betty was yammering on about how she just loved the tail end of hurricane season and how it seemed to her such a lovely, dishonest time. Miss Betty had had a party the night before and the house smelled of fish, perfume, and alcohol. There were crumbled napkins and dirty glasses still in the living room and Miss Betty told Norma to recycle any empty bottles from the liquor cabinet. The bottles were standing on a marble side table under a picture of Miss Betty's great-grandfather. Miss Betty had the good stuff and there was a lot still left. As Norma passed, following Miss Betty to the back bathrooms, the floor rumbled and the bottles shook and clinked against each other.

Sometimes Norma walked into a house with just a little mess and she'd wonder why the woman couldn't clean up herself, why she had to hire someone to do her cleaning. Donna had explained it once and Norma figured she understood as well as anyone: There were times when a person needed somebody's help to get back to ground zero just so they could get on with their lives. Some did their own dishes, stripped their own beds, bothered about their own laundry, but it always took people like Norma and Donna to know that behind every microwave lay cobwebs, under every refrigerator was dirt.

Most people along the Mississippi coast weren't entirely comfortable with white maids. They figured something was wrong with a white woman who would be a maid, but Norma could tell that Miss Betty had gotten used to her and to Donna, maybe because they did not look at all like Miss Betty. Norma and Donna could have been mistaken for sisters. They both had heavy, hanging breasts, narrow hips and dark hair. Norma often told Miss Betty that she and Donna were like Lavern and Shirley from that old TV show—always laughing and getting into trouble, spending more time with each other than with anybody else.

Cleaning other people's houses was better than working third shift at the shirt factory, a dismal place with no windows and no air-conditioning. The outside of the building was painted with pretty, false windows and planters, and wisteria bloomed eternally over fake open doorways. The other girls who worked there were all younger than Norma, and they reminded her of all the mistakes she had made. On breaks and at lunchtime, she sat outside in the shade, smoking and watching them eating their hamburgers, going on and on about plans that would never materialize, houses that would never be bought, men who never were what they pretended to be. These girls still laughed and their laughter still sounded like giggling, and even if they smoked, the sound of their giggles came out clear and sing-songy. Norma had met Donna at the factory. They were about the same age and they were put to work side by side—Donna doing buttons, Norma zippers.

Norma put baby Charlie down in his car seat, and then she set to work on Miss Betty's bathroom. Norma was tired, but she was used to waking up feeling heavy and hung-over, working and waiting for the end of her shift, waiting for another drink to give her a few hours worth of light-headedness. She thought everyone worked through their days this way. She could not remember spending the waking hours of her life any other way and she felt she had finally become what she was meant to become—a tired old woman. At least she knew who she was and what she was.

Miss Betty had already packed her bags. She was dressed up, ready to go out, trying to hook a gold bracelet around her wrist. All summer Miss Betty had felt smug, telling everybody how good her bone density was ever since she had been shopping at that expensive health food store at the corner downtown.

"I was sorry to hear about Donna," Miss Betty said, looking up from her bracelet. "How's Charlie?" Without touching him, Miss Betty bent over to examine Charlie in his car seat on the bedroom floor. She neither smiled nor frowned. Miss Betty did not say so now, but she was of the belief that the reason there was so much E. coli in the world was because there were too many people with too many pets and too many babies and there was just too much "dookie." She had used that word—*dookie*—when she told this theory once to Norma and Donna. That was before there was Charlie. Later, over a pitcher of beer, Norma and Donna had laughed long and loud, repeating the way Miss Betty had said *dookie.*

"Charlie's doing real good," Norma said, on her knees, scrubbing out the tub. She went on to tell Miss Betty what a wonderful woman and good friend Donna had been, how such a thing ought never to have happened, how she hated to think of Donna all alone out there on the highway in the middle of the night, it raining and all, and Miss Betty interrupted and said, "I know, I know. Why on earth didn't she just take a cab? Drinking so much then driving. All those times she used to call in saying she was too depressed or too tired to work. What was it last? Oh yes. She said you were both laid up with sick-headaches." Miss Betty shook her head and Norma thought she saw her smile. "Now we know, don't we? We know all right. She was just hung over. It could make a person livid."

The bathroom cleaner stung Norma's eyes, and even though the air conditioning was on, she had to open a window for air. Norma tried to think of something to say back to Miss Betty then, but already Miss Betty was going on now about her *evacuation* and how she'd be out for the day and for all week that week staying with relatives somewhere *inland*, around Magnolia. *Do be careful not to touch a Louis-something chair, Mrs. R. P. Smith sat in it and broke it last night*, and *could Norma get rid of those sunflowers over there, wilting in the corner? They smelled like dog piss*. Miss Betty swore at the clasp she still could not clasp, stuck out her arm toward Norma, who, without a word, fastened the bracelet.

"I hope *you* have a place to go," Miss Betty said, her breath smelling like mangoes. It was understood: Miss Betty was getting out and she wanted, no, *needed*, Norma to look after the house. Norma had her own key. Donna had once confessed to Norma that she wondered about Miss Betty and her kind—those women who lived closest to the water, women who talked about teas and lawn service and "building" their wardrobes. Donna had wondered out loud how such women spent the minutes of each day and what all they thought on. They had time to take naps and sit in a fancy chair to just think about the seasons or the way the wind blows curtains and changes the shadows in a room. They had time to forget their sadnesses, to be happy, and to laugh.

"We're not down low," Miss Betty said. "Did I ever tell you my great-grandfather built this house? See that rise out front? I like to think he knew it would save us from Camille," Miss Betty smiled, as if she really believed only poor people got killed.

Norma cleaned quickly that day, thinking about Miss Betty's party alcohol, telling baby Charlie about what all a person could do with baking soda and Windex, and wondering all the while what Donna's last thoughts had been, if she had thought of Charlie or even of Norma herself. Norma couldn't help but wonder about the details of Donna's accident, which parts of her *exactly* lay broken in the street and how much blood there had been. As Norma stripped the beds, then made them back up again, she hoped that an angel had come down with the rain to hold her friend's crushed head while she lay in all that wet, twisted wreckage.

Miss Betty liked her bottles dusted before they were put away, and as Norma worked through the bar, she could hear herself thinking as she drank: *You deserve this drink because your head is numb and you've lost your best friend. And you deserve another because your husband's out of work and another because you don't want to go home.*

Norma and Donna always saved big houses like Miss Betty's along the waterfront for the end of the day, because afterwards, they could go down to the beach and walk on the flat part of the shore. Norma first told Donna about her first husband, Catch, there on that beach. Already Norma missed looking at Donna's bare feet in the salt water—her toenails painted red for the winter. They'd wipe the sand from their feet, then go up a ways to a bar at the corner of the street. It was then, after work, with Donna, waiting for drinks, when they smoked and talked about how bone-tired they were, that Norma would think to herself how much she needed to laugh again just to wake up, just to feel alive. Then the drinks would come and they'd toast something or somebody and they'd take their first sip and there would be a moment of silent, forgetful relief and it was in this quiet, holy second that Norma would always let go with a laugh because she felt safe then—like with Donna and with that drink under the canopy of their cigarette smoke, everybody and everything was going to be alright.

Norma couldn't clean any of the other houses that week. They were all too big and lonely without Donna, and before she went to work her shift at the factory, Norma went back to Miss Betty's house every day, not to clean, but to sit outside on the porch with Charlie. When she saw Sam it was only to say she'd already eaten or not to wait up or Charlie needed more diapers. She never waited around long enough to hear his response.

It was raining every afternoon now, and one day, outside on Miss Betty's porch, Norma held Charlie in her lap, and feeling heavy and light-headed, she rocked him and told him about Camille. Norma had been fifteen when Camille hit. Some said the worst part was all the noise, but for Norma, the worst part was afterwards—the boats and bodies hanging from all those naked trees and the enormous effort it took to keep on living just when you didn't think you had anything more left in you.

It was like that now. It felt like after Camille. Ever since Donna had died, Norma felt as though the world had stopped and she didn't know how to get the strength back to start it spinning again.

Sitting out on Miss Betty's porch that day, Norma took another sip from her drink and looked out at the Gulf, which was the color of Miss Betty's slate roof. She knew then that it really was the end of her friend Donna's life and that there was no getting her back, but it felt so much like the end of something else too. Drinking had killed Donna, and Norma knew at one point she would have to quit. But she did not want to quit, not yet, not now. It had been a month since the accident and Norma realized she had not laughed. Donna had said once that not being able to laugh was like being too weak to think of strength. Norma looked at Charlie, asleep in his car seat on the porch, then she rocked him awake and lifted him up to show him the dark, bourbon-colored sky, explaining to him why he would never be able to drink it all, even though someday she knew he would want to.

Norma woke up to the sun going down. It was windy out and the air felt yellow with the cool, but it didn't smell like rain.

Charlie was gone.

The tomato sauce smell coming from Miss Betty's kitchen filled the house with a warm, dark odor and Norma thought of how she would have to remind herself to open all the windows to air the place out before Miss Betty came back. Charlie was asleep in his car seat on top of the kitchen table. Plastic grocery bags ballooned all around Sam's feet as he stood at the stove, stirring.

"You just left me out there?" Norma said.

"You deserved to be left outside during a hurricane, Norma. You put that baby in danger. You think about that."

"I need something to drink."

Sam put a glass of something in front of her.

"Iced tea," he said.

They both looked at the glass.

"You can snap out of it now, Norma," he yelled. "Don't you see?" He spoke quietly then. "You've got to give the three of us a chance first before you go on and give up on everything and everybody."

Norma didn't say anything as she stood without moving.

The TV in the kitchen was on and the local weatherman was standing out on the beach without a raincoat, saying that strong winds were headed that way and a hurricane might not be far behind.

Sam cleared his throat, then he told her how he had driven by Miss Betty's in his pick-up and had seen Norma passed out in the rocking chair on the porch. She had managed—just barely—to keep hold of the baby, who, with a soggy, dirty diaper, had been crying for who knew how long.

"I'll make a deal with you," Sam said finally. "I'll quit drinking too, right now, if you quit your drinking. We can quit it the same way we did with the blow."

"It's not that bad. I just wanted to feel good again."

"You can't let yourself fall apart, Norma. You're not even trying." Sam looked at her then. "Not with me and not with yourself." She thought he might get a beer then, but he did not.

"Charlie needs you. I need you and you need us." Sam paused and looked at Charlie asleep. "We'll do what we have to. Meetings. Whatever. We got Charlie to think of now. I ain't never had a kid, and I'm not fucking up like I seen some do."

"So now you think I been fucking up." Norma felt her face get red.

"That's not what I meant."

They both stared at each other. Norma wanted to leave the room, the house, get in her car and drive to Alabama—

anywhere east or west, it didn't matter, but the storm shutters were shut and the rain was coming down hard.

Sam limped over to her. She felt sticky now with a cold sweat. He said he would kneel down if he could, but with the cast and all, he awkwardly held her hand instead. Sam's rough palm was warm and dry and Norma allowed herself to fall into a chair.

"You know when I fell off the roof of that video store and didn't die, I felt like I got a second chance. Now I think I might be getting me enough computer skills so I can get some decent work. I've already got a lead on a job selling water systems. I won't have to keep killing myself putting up crappy little stores and you won't have to work at that factory."

"I need a cigarette," Norma said, looking around the room.

Sam put a cigarette in his mouth, lit it, then gave it to Norma. She took a long drag and considered the possibilities.

"Donna." Sam shook his head then. "She didn't get another chance."

A reporter was on TV talking to a woman at the grocery store. The woman was saying how much energy she had, knowing a hurricane might hit. She'd cleaned her house and now she was polishing all her silver.

Absentmindedly, Norma touched her own hair. The roots were coming out gray. She hadn't done anything to it since that day she and Donna took off and colored each other's hair in the kitchen sink. Donna had died that night, a blond.

"I look like a raccoon," Norma said.

"You look damned good," Sam said. "And you know what else? You're strong enough for what's ahead. You might not know it, but I do. What's that the Brits say? Chin up."

Norma sipped from her glass. The sweet iced tea made her think of God and the coast. She bent down and kissed the top of Charlie's head. His hair smelled of everything.

Norma wanted to tell Sam to screw it all, to sit back down with her and drink and laugh for the rest of the evening, till the storm blew the pretty little roof off of Miss Betty's old house. That's what she and Catch would have done and he would have called it their own private hurricane party. But that wretched time would come *after* the storm and Norma didn't want to be sick or passed out or in need of another drink.

They listened to the weatherman's wind-snatched voice on the TV, a line of cars behind him, slowly moving north. This was just a tropical storm, he said. Another mass was moving their way and it was gathering into a Cat 3 hurricane that could turn into something worse.

Norma sat staring at the black and blue computer instructions Sam had scribbled up and down his cast. She saw something about *saving instructions.*

"I'll go put some towels under the doors," she said, getting up slower than usual. "For the leaks."

The electricity went out, a wall of rain came down hard, and Charlie woke up crying. All the noise spooked him and he howled louder and longer than ever. Norma rocked him until he calmed down, and over his whimpers they could hear the rain on the roof and against the windows. The shutters shook. Sam got out flashlights, batteries and candles, then filled up all the bathtubs just in case they lost the water too.

They ate by candlelight in Miss Betty's big dining room. From Norma's lap, Charlie watched the flickering light. Norma hadn't known how hungry she was.

"That's one of my favorite sounds," Sam said as Norma chewed. "The sound of you eating something you really like."

The dark house and all that rain made them both nervous and polite with each other, like they were on a first date they'd never really had.

Finally the storm blew past. Sam found a battery operated radio, and when he turned it on, the weatherman was warning everybody that hurricane season wasn't over yet and that there were predictions that the "big" one was still to come. Fate or luck had turned this hurricane into a nasty tropical depression with gale winds.

They brought Charlie into the living room and they pulled open the shutters to have a look outside. Tree branches littered the yard and the Gulf looked choppy and gray.

"Maybe this time next year, you'll be an assistant manager somewheres," Norma said, sighing, beginning to think now of wanting a drink.

"Maybe we'll get us a house of our own. A brick one," he said. "We've had a string of bad luck is all. But I can feel it changing. I can."

They were both of them looking out the window and Norma hoped they weren't just dreaming. Then she felt Sam's lips touching the back of her neck. She breathed out and settled her head back on his chest.

She recognized the vast stretch of white beach before them, the two sprawling live oaks, the telephone wires, the slick highway, and the possibility that her life would never really change no matter what new job Sam got or where they moved, would in fact, always be just what it was now. She was born on the Gulf, lived on the Gulf, and she would, most likely, die there. Norma had never thought much about why she lived where she lived just as she had not thought much about being with Sam all these years, not until Donna died, not until now. But standing there, looking out Miss Betty's window, Norma felt just then a vague sense of relief that at least she and Sam were not landlocked. At least here there was always something or at least the chance of something wonderful, terrible, or dangerous coming at them and it was up to them to see it through. She knew she did not really need a drink just then—didn't quite yet *have* to have one, and all at once, for just that moment, she felt less heavy.

Norma's breath was fogging up the window and she made a mark with her finger. She thought how funny it was that just standing there breathing could make an actual mark, as though by just being alive she made some kind of difference. She knew there was a chance she would forget this moment, this good feeling of not needing but of just being. She hoped she would not forget. Sam reached over, and with his index finger, he drew a heart. Just then, Charlie stirred in his car seat on the floor, and Norma and Sam stared at each other with the same expression on their faces as though they had finally gotten the same joke. Sam picked Charlie up and held him toward the window. Norma breathed again then she made another heart next to Sam's, then another and another, and with each heart Norma made, the baby kicked and giggled, and as the window caught the last bit of light from the sun going down, Sam smiled at Norma laughing.

THE SWING

Catch lit a joint and smoked it as he drove past the Gulf Coast Pak & Ship, which still had its sun-faded *WE SHIP FOR THE HOLIDAYS* sign up from last year. It was Friday, Christmas Eve, and he was going to fetch his holiday bonus from Mr. Zimmer in the big yellow house, his last paycheck for the week. Squinting from all the light coming off the Gulf, Catch smiled, and his fingers slid along the steering wheel, anticipating those crisp, new bills Mr. Zimmer would count out from his silver money clip.

He passed the old-people's home, and through his open window he could smell the stuffing and sweet potatoes cooking. He always did like mushy food, and he laughed thinking about what a good old person he would be. He snuffed out his joint, slipping the charred nub back into a Ziploc bag for later, and reached into the passenger seat for some cheese crackers and beef jerky. He still had the open box of Satsuma oranges and divinity cookies from Mrs. Gimbel and the sugared pecans from Mrs. Anderson. He'd save those for later. A man on a bicycle wearing a Santa hat waved, and Catch waved back.

In the Zimmers' drive, Catch slammed his truck door shut, straightened his hat, and laughed out loud at the Christmas display on the lawn next door: Santa was riding his sleigh, holding a whip to the reindeer, while two white wire angels with flashlights stood in front of the sleigh, looking like those people who guide planes in for landings. The Zimmers didn't go for outdoor holiday decorations, and this, combined with their last name, had made Catch think at first that they were Jewish, but it turned out they were Lutherans.

Around back the Zimmers' grown daughter was swimming laps in the heated pool, steam dancing off the surface of the water. She slogged back and forth without once stopping or looking up. The daughter's young son sat in the wheelbarrow parked next to the pool, reading a science book bigger than his head.

"Hey, partner," Catch said.

"Hey," the boy said, his mouth going back into the little green scarf someone had wound around his neck. What was his name again? He was tiny and blond, his eyes were big like his mother's, and his mother's mother's. He looked like he wanted to smile but couldn't; like he thought he had to ask permission.

"Excited about all the presents you're going to get?"

The boy nodded. There was silence, and then the boy asked, "How are you?"

Catch wasn't accustomed to a seven-year-old talking this way, and he had to get used to the boy again. Teddy—that was his name. This kid wasn't stupid and not a bit shy, but if the Zimmers weren't careful, he was going to turn into a wormy, womany sissy. Catch liked to give it to him straight. "How am I? you say? Could be better. Could be worse. I'm still standing. Still breathing. I call that a victory."

Teddy looked curiously at Catch, then tucked his mouth back into his scarf.

Catch inspected the green yard he'd seeded with rye grass a month earlier. He'd learned to anticipate what homeowners needed. There were a lot of house-proud people in this neighborhood. Catch could fit five trailers inside the Zimmers' house. He didn't know where all the money that had landed on this street came from, but he figured either out-of-state sugar or oil. Nobody ever made that kind of money in Mississippi; you had to leave, make your money, then bring it back with you. Some of these folks lived on the Gulf year-round, but there were others, like the Zimmers, who came down for the winter. They needed a local to keep up the house and the lawn. Catch often wondered why the Zimmers kept coming back here, why they didn't keep a place in, say, California.

The little porch on the martin house was rotting off. The birdhouse was made to look like the big house, and Catch felt obligated to make it look as nice, but Mr. Zimmer wanted him to concentrate on the big jobs: trimming the boxwood around the tennis court and cutting back the line of bamboo. Last Christmas, Mrs. Zimmer had ordered a fancy swing from a catalogue, but with so much on her mind, she'd left it outside on the ground for a month, and after several heavy rains, the seat had cupped and split. Catch had told Mrs. Zimmer he could make a better swing himself anyway. Leave it to him; he'd get around to it. He'd even picked the perfect live oak to hang it in.

The Zimmers' kitchen door opened, and oniony smells wafted out; there was Mrs. Zimmer, looking frantic.

"Catch," she said. "Oh, I'm so glad you're here." She gave him an envelope. "That's for the month and there's your bonus, too. Now, I know it's your day off, but I need you today and tonight. Could you help? Please? The lawn needs mowing again, and we can't put up the tree by ourselves. We've got guests coming over at six. And tomorrow's Christmas. I just don't know if I can manage. Do you want to come in for coffee? Have you had breakfast?"

Mrs. Zimmer wasn't quite like the other retired women. Lady up the street wouldn't even let Catch inside her house; at lunchtime she opened up a can of Vienna sausages and dumped them out on a paper plate, then handed the plate to Catch with some saltines, like she was feeding a cat. Catch was a white yard man. He wondered what that woman had fed the black men who'd worked for her before him.

Catch tipped his hat, said he'd had breakfast, and sure, he could take the mower for a once-around.

Riding the John Deere, he lit the rest of his joint: just enough to make the morning feel like a celebration. The air was cold and hurt Catch's teeth. At least it wasn't August or September, when he would have been sweating into his eyes. Riding a mower and smoking some weed the day before Christmas suited Catch just fine. Pot was the only drug he liked to mess with. His former boss at the lumberyard had had a bad cocaine habit. Catch could deal with just about anything but that. One morning his boss had knocked the cowboy hat off Catch's head and lit into him, yelling and waving a knife. Catch punched him in the face, good and solid, then picked up his hat and left. That was the end of that job.

After Catch had finished mowing, he went back up to the house to see what else Mrs. Zimmer needed. She stepped outside, holding on to the screen door so it wouldn't slam. Catch thought she seemed to be moving much better after the hip surgery. She had put on a few pounds, but the weight looked good on her. So did the tangerine lipstick and the blue flowered dress. Mrs. Zimmer didn't study Catch the way the other old women did, the way Catch was used to being studied. He knew what they thought of him. He lived alone; he drank. Some knew about the dope, but most didn't. Everyone knew he was quick to anger. He got into fights. He got kicked out of places. Some might have felt sorry for him. He knew he wasn't *happy* happy. He knew people studied his kind of not happiness—he didn't want to call it "*un*happiness" or "depression" or "post-traumatic stress disorder": he'd been like this before and after the two tours in Vietnam.

"I know this is your day off, Catch, but can you help with the tree, too?"

"Help" meant put it up. Mrs. Zimmer liked to tell people Catch "helped" with the yard and the gardening when, in fact, he did it all. He never bothered correcting her, of course.

The tree lay on the back porch, or what Mrs. Zimmer called "the gallery," and Catch knelt down on the cold marble and screwed last year's stand onto it. Upright, the tree was small and bushy. He wondered how much the old lady had paid. She'd probably been ripped off.

"Oh, it's perfect," she said as he hauled it in from the porch.

He would have gotten a bigger one, taller. Why else have twelve-foot ceilings like that?

"Can you put on the strings of lights too? We're only doing red and silver decorations this year."

Catch opened the lights and colored balls and put them all on the tree. At the last minute, the old woman gave him one more box to hang: twelve sea-glass ornaments, a gift from some woman named Nelia.

"Oh, that's perfect Catch, perfect. I don't know how you do it." She handed him a package.

"Thank you, Mrs. Z. You oughtn't have," he said, thinking the bundle felt too light for a ham.

"I was wondering if you could put it on. For tonight. We're hoping you could play Santa at the party. It wouldn't be Christmas without Santa."

Catch opened the package. It was a lot of red inside.

"You'll be a Victorian Saint Nick," she said, staring down at the red velvet suit in his hands. "It wasn't a cheapie."

Outside, the daughter was still swimming laps in the pool. It made Catch's head hurt just watching her. Why did people make their lives more difficult than they already were?

Catch drove home to eat and think. He lived in a trailer park but was saving up for a nice brick ranch house on the bay. He wanted his own dock and a motorboat, so he could go fishing first thing in the morning, maybe take the boat to Wolf River if he had a mind to.

He boiled three hotdogs, and still carrying the Santa package, took a seat on the lone aluminum chair out front. There was no grass, but he kept the ground swept. He didn't mind the passing trains so much anymore, not when he thought of how he would have the boat soon enough. Between his trailer and the train tracks, he grew tomatoes and peppers in tires, coffee cans, and milk jugs cut in half. He breathed in the smell of sweet olive, magnolia and pine, then popped open a beer. He knew he drank too much, because lately he felt old in the mornings. One day he'd quit.

Part of the beard hung from the package, tickling his thigh. He opened the box. The beard was big and curly, but they'd skimped on the boots: vinyl flaps that strapped onto a regular shoe. There were some things that just shouldn't be.

Mrs. Zimmer was waiting for him on the front porch, and when she saw Catch in the suit but still wearing his work boots, she said no no. She noticed things like shoes. He strapped on the flaps.

Mrs. Zimmer led Catch into the house through the front door. The living room was all lit up, and there were more people there than he'd expected: older people with no kids, neighbors from front and back and sideways. He mowed lawns for many of them, maybe one square mile all together. Shrimp and oysters on the half shell sat for the taking in a big crystal bowl full of ice. He didn't know why the Zimmers put out such a fine spread for people he was sure didn't appreciate it. Why didn't they just do like that old man down the street did? On Christmas day, he gave any relative who came by a hundred dollars. Catch got fifty and a pie. No fuss, no muss.

"Pardon me," Teddy said. He had a gap in his smile where his two front teeth were out; the new teeth were coming in crooked. "Are you Santa Claus?'

"You bet, partner. How about you tell me what you want for Christmas."

"I think you're supposed to sit down first," the boy said. Mr. Zimmer came into the room with two drinks. "But not in that chair. Grandmother doesn't like for people to sit on that chair. It's from some other century, not this one."

Mr. Zimmer told Teddy to get Santa some gumbo, and he led Catch to a big leather wing-back chair and put a hot toddy in his hand. Then Mr. Zimmer counted out three twenties, a ten, and a five from the wad of money in his clip. No wallet, this guy. Catch tucked the cash into his red velvet suit and sipped the toddy. He overheard a lot of talk about the hurricanes they'd had in Florida that year: Charlie and Frances. "They had to gut Emma's condo because of the mold," some woman said to Mrs. Zimmer. Teddy came with a cup of gumbo. Catch took a taste. Someone in that kitchen knew how to burn a roux good. Lord Almighty! Right now, he could drink up the afternoon.

One wall of the room was all glass, and Catch could see the whole Gulf of Mexico from where he sat. Even though the water was polluted, it was pretty to look at and think on. When he was married, he and his ex-wife Norma would spread out a blanket and picnic there on the beach, smoke a little weed, then lie back, close their eyes, and just listen. It was only a drab little spot of sand, but the sound of the water was just the same as it would have been on some Hawaiian island. Those were the best nights in Pass Christian—you all but forgot about the poisons in the water.

Mr. Zimmer plopped the kid on Catch's lap. Catch knew he smelled of weed, and what with the hot toddy and the gumbo on his bad stomach, he hoped to God he didn't get sick.

"It's Christmas Eve," the boy said. "Shouldn't you be working?"

"I am, son. And what do you want for Christmas?"

The boy shrugged. "I don't know."

Catch looked around the room, where everything and everyone sparkled. Someday it would all belong to this little kid. He wouldn't even have to ask for it. It was just automatic, a fact of life. It would be his. "I suppose you don't have to want anything," Catch said. "Used to be all I wanted for Christmas was snow."

"I sort of already know what I'm going to get. Santa always brings me lots of new books and clothes, a new coat, and maybe a ball. And Mom gives me candy and new stationery for thank you notes. Last year it was Curious George." He sniffled, then reached into his pocket and pulled out some blue Kleenex covered in penguins.

"Well what is it you want? Hell kid, you got everything right here."

The boy looked at Catch with a you-don't-get-it-do-you? look. "There aren't any kids to play with."

"Maybe you're just a little homesick," Catch said as the boy blew his nose. "I heard a nasty rumor. I heard you *like* Chicago."

"I live there. You ever been?"

"Once, in 1992. Too many people. Too many people where I'm at now, too. I'll move farther up North."

"Norther than the North pole?"

"Ah . . . yeah."

"You don't like people?"

"No real need for them. Look. Kid. Ted. Let's figure out what you want for Christmas, huh?"

"I don't know what's wrong with my Mom. She acts mad all the time, ever since Dad left."

Catch looked across the room at the kid's mom, a good-looking woman, her skin saggy, not from age, but from weight loss. She'd married and divorced some Chicago Yankee who used to show up on holidays with all those fruit-named gadgets, like Apple and Blackberry: little computers that turned into phones; phones that took pictures. Now he wasn't showing up anymore.

"All my life I've been trying to get away from rooms like these," the daughter said to some neighbors, her eyes circled with the red indentations from her swim goggles. Someone needed to feed that poor woman a plate full of red beans and rice with some good andouille sausage, or maybe just a steak.

"She's just disappointed is all," Catch said to Teddy. "Haven't you ever been disappointed?"

The kid thought for a minute. "I went to a birthday party once, and they didn't have cake."

"That's what I'm talking about. Sucks, don't it."

The kid showed Catch a clip attached to the buttonhole of his shirt. The clip looked like it might hold a mitten to a coat sleeve. "This is where I keep my lucky rock. I clip it here. Then it sucks out the luckiness, which gets into my coat, which is next to my sleeve, which is next to my arm skin, and I get charged with the luck, and then I am powerful."

"All right. Now you're thinking," Catch said. "Anything else on your mind?"

"Why *do* people swing their arms when they walk?"

"Jesus, kid. I don't know. Helps them keep moving, I guess."

"Making your list, checking it twice?" Mr. Zimmer said, putting another hot toddy in Catch's hand. God bless him.

"You have a lot of fur on your hands," the boy said to Catch. His nails were dirty too. They were always dirty from work the day before, and the day before that.

"Yeah well. So what do you want for Christmas?"

The boy shrugged. "A surprise is all."

"Come on, kid. Ask for something big. Your granddaddy—I mean, I can get my elves to make you anything. How about a BB gun?"

"I'm not allowed."

Catch could hear an old woman he used to work for giving somebody details he didn't want to hear about her woman-surgery. She sighed loudly, shook her drink, and said, "Really, at my age, all you've got left is your posture and your jewels."

"All right, then. How about a treehouse?"

"Grandmother says it will ruin her view."

Catch nodded and gulped his drink. Mrs. Zimmer hobbled toward them, smiling. There were lines on her soft, pale face where she'd been smiling all her life. "Santa, please have something more to eat, or another drink."

"No, Mrs. Z. I've got too much to do tonight. You and I both know I'm on duty." Catch winked and then lifted the boy from his lap. The boy whispered in Catch's ear, "I think my grandmother's hard of hearing."

"Well, that happens when folks get old," he whispered back to the boy. "We lose stuff along the way."

§

The wind off the Gulf was colder now, and as Catch drove back up the highway, still wearing the Santa suit, he wished he had saved the rest of that joint. He considered going to the casino—maybe he could double the money in his pocket. He pulled off onto a quiet street, stopped the car, and got out to vomit. He puked up all of it: gumbo, oysters, shrimp, everything. A dog came trotting by and started eating up the mess, which made him puke all over again. He got some on his suit, and he wondered briefly how he would clean it.

Catch stopped at a gas-station pay phone to call a girl he knew, but he got her machine. "Hey," he said into the phone after the beep. "It's just me. I was wondering if you was at home or what." When he got back in the car, he regretted the call and headed for the McDonald's drive-through, the only place still open at dinnertime on Christmas Eve. Hoping to settle his stomach, he ordered a big dinner, paid, and drove off without it. Halfway home, he realized what he'd done, and he went back.

"Pardon me," he said to the girl taking orders. After he'd said it, he remembered these were the same words Teddy had used. The words sounded strange to Catch in his own voice. He explained to the girl that he'd forgotten his food and tried to laugh at himself. As he waited at the window for her to put his order together again, he looked inside to see his ex-wife, Norma, standing at the counter. She was wearing a blue velour jogging suit and ordering, he was certain, a Filet-O-Fish sandwich. It was what she always ordered when she was high on something. No way did he want to see her now, smelly and dressed as he was.

After he got his food, he parked across from the public park facing the Gulf and he started in on his fries. Used to be he and Norma would swing on those playground swings and walk that very beach. She'd left after she hooked up with her dealer, Catch's old boss at the lumberyard. She was high and swearing up a mean streak the day she walked out, throwing her things into a big plastic garbage bag, yelling until her voice finally got cut off by the door as it slammed shut behind her.

A car passed on the street, and Catch could feel the thumping rap music in his loins. Some of the kids inside the car threw Mardi Gras beads, which hit the hood of Catch's pickup. People around here, they got a little money, and they went out and bought cellphones, DVD players, and sound systems for their cars. As far as Catch could tell, it all landed up at the pawn shops near the casinos.

He unwrapped his first burger and then bit into it. Well fuck. There was no meat, just bread, sauce, and lettuce. The other two were the same. *Ha ha to you too*, he thought, sure this was some damn joke that McDonald's girl had played on him. Maybe Norma had even had something to do with it. This stuff didn't just happen on accident. Nothing just happened.

Catch turned the key to the ignition. He had in mind to go back and ram the place with Norma in it. He hit his steering wheel hard, honking the horn. In the distance, a horn honked back. Dogs barked, and someone yelled, "Merry Christmas!" He caught a glimpse of his fake white beard in the rearview mirror, the curls dirty and sagging now around his neck. He took a deep breath and let it out with a cough, then turned off the engine, opened the windows, and looked again at the Gulf.

Back in Khe Sanh, his best friend had had a Zippo lighter engraved with a motto: "If I had a farm in Vietnam and a home in hell, I'd sell my farm and go home." Catch had kept the lighter after he'd zipped up his friend in a body bag.

Catch thought about what the Mississippi Sound was made of. There it was, half the country's rivers spilling their guts out into the Gulf of Mexico, the ocean waters taking on the world's poisons, the whole of it creeping back with the tide, inching its way toward land like so many injured soldiers crawling back home. Dying waters, but not dead yet, going back and forth, up and down the beach. And every now and again, a hurricane came along, and those sorry waves partied hard on the land, flattening beach houses, wiping the earth clean.

And slowly Catch started missing his ex-wife; or not so much Norma, as just having a wife. A buddy of his had told him once about how French girls had come in groups to the Mississippi Gulf Coast back in the 1700s, chaperoned by Ursuline nuns. They were called the "*casquette* girls," because they came with suitcases to marry French settlers. Better than mail-order brides, these French girls were carefully selected, skilled, and pious, and some of the proudest Creoles trace their ancestry to them. They made a movie about it years ago, a musical in black and white. Looking out at the horizon, Catch felt like one of those early settlers now, and just as those brides had come to all those lonely men, he hoped some big idea would come to him and make his life better.

On Christmas morning, in the dark of predawn, Catch snuck into the Zimmers' backyard, a knife in one hand and his flashlight in the other. He'd gotten a good, solid board, weatherproofed and treated. He had good rope too, thick and sturdy, and he carried all this in the pack on his back. He would have worked faster without the dope, but still, in a little over an hour, he put the swing together right. Recalling how the boy's knees hit him midshin, he adjusted the height just so.

"Oh Catch. Catch." Mrs. Zimmer stood on her back gallery with a tray of rolls and coffee. She poured him a cup and put it in his hands. "Merry Christmas. I'm so glad you stopped by."

They watched the boy swing higher and higher, the toes of his red footed pajamas almost touching the tree's leaves.

"Do you think that branch is secure?" Mrs. Zimmer said.

"Oh, it'll hold."

"Santa knew, didn't he?" Mrs. Zimmer said, smiling up at him.

Catch would always remember this moment. He thought so even then. And when he'd come back a year later to see all the wreckage from Katrina, to see how the boardwalk from the Gulf had landed in the backyard, along with the bits and pieces of furniture and house, Catch would stand there in wonder to find that swing still hanging from that tree, unharmed.

Catch cupped his hands over his mouth and shouted to Teddy, "What's it look like from up there?"

"You and Grandmother look like ants," the boy shouted back.

"Suits us just fine."

Mrs. Zimmer touched his arm. "Do you think you could help me throw out all these boxes? The presents I had shipped for everybody came so overpackaged."

"Now? Won't the kid see, then start asking questions about . . . you know, Santa and all?"

"Oh, I hadn't thought about that. But surely he doesn't still believe. Do you think?"

They watched the boy slow the swing down, scraping the grass with his toe, then push off again.

"Tell you what. I'll get those when he goes back into the house."

"Catch, you're wonderful. I don't know how you do it."

"Mrs. Z., about the Santa suit: I need to get it cleaned before I return it."

Mrs. Zimmer shook her head. "Keep it, Catch. You're a natural. Save it for next year."

He laughed and said, "Now, just wait a minute, Mrs. Z."

But Mrs. Zimmer touched his arm and Catch put his hand on top of hers. This was before Katrina took away the Zimmers and the town and all those other people he'd just gotten to liking. This was before. And for that moment, the two of them stood there on the back gallery, smelling the jasmine growing up alongside the house and watching the boy swing.

HOLIDAY WORLD

They lost me on purpose. They always do. They come here to Holiday World, knowing I hate Splashin' Safari, so they leave me around the Jungle Jets. Then after they wash themselves off, they slink away.

We came up here to Indiana from Pass Christian, Mississippi, after Katrina washed away everything. We're staying with people my mom wants me to call my aunt and uncle. FEMA and the TV news people call us *Displaced Persons* even though we have a place. Had a place. The people we're staying with? I can tell they don't want me to call them Aunt or Uncle. I can tell they're tired of us. And I can tell you this right now; I'm sick of them too. All they eat is cereal. We've been through a hurricane, and what do they do? They take us to a water park.

My name is Billy. You want a description of them? My dad's wearing cut-offs. He's on the rides. He's the first to go. My mom's name is Anne and I don't know what color her hair is. I know what color it's supposed to be: brown, like mine, but she dyes it red and black and there's some purple in it today. What do you mean *distinctive* clothing? She's got a bathing suit on. A one-piece with a pair of cut-offs and yellow flip-flops. No, no hat. No glasses. No lifejacket or hair ribbons.

They try and make the cement here look like sand. See? You can see the indents of shells pressed in. The concrete next to The Wave is supposed to look like a beach, like a disguise. It's all pretend. That's what they say. That's why you call this place Lost Parents and not Missing Children, isn't it? Everyone's trying to be funny. Everyone's pretending. I'll tell you straight out, they're not coming to get me. Here? They only look for kids, not parents. It's like a safe house.

All they play is Beatles music here, too. Why's that? *Shake it up baby. Twist and shout.* I miss jazz. I miss blues.

My mom? I told you the last place seen: Jungle Jets. Look for her. You'll see her walking. She just walks around and around the water, never going on the rides. She'll be carrying a Big Gulp. She drinks the free soda and gets her hands and feet wet. She walks and walks all around the water, as if we haven't seen enough water to last a lifetime.

PLACE VALUE

After Katrina drowned their house on the Gulf, Teddy's grandparents came north and moved in with Teddy and his mother in Chicago. They only had the four suitcases, and his grandmother tried to sound playful when she announced they were in a homeless state. But that was OK because she loved Teddy's city where you could get anything any time, including culture, which she said she planned to consume like shrimp or lump crabmeat at least three times a day.

Teddy and his mother lived in a modern steel and glass building overlooking Lake Michigan. His grandparents slept in the guestroom Teddy's father had used as an office. After the divorce, his father moved to New York because he had gotten an even better job, and, it was assumed, a better life. He was very good at managing money, Teddy's mother explained to Teddy once, not so good at managing people. She said this in such a way that made the ice in her glass shift.

After they moved in, Teddy's grandfather mostly talked on the phone to the insurance people and watched the news alone, staring at replays of the pink and red swirls that had been the hurricane paths Teddy learned about in science. Over dinner Teddy listened to the three of them talk about the water and food that was not getting delivered to the survivors, the trees and concrete that wasn't getting moved in the two weeks that had already passed.

Then Catch, the man who helped his grandparents with everything, called from Pass Christian. His grandfather had to sit down to listen. Later, Teddy found out what Catch said exactly: *"I'm standing in front of what was your house. It's mostly gone like everything else, but you still have a structure and part of a roof."*

Teddy's grandfather hung up and told Teddy's mother what she had to do—she had to go down and see what, if anything, could be salvaged. Teddy watched his mother nod as though she were in a dream. Teddy's mother had never volunteered for anything—not even for bake sales or car washes at his school. She said other mothers could do that sort of thing, not her.

To ready herself to go to Mississippi in a convoy of volunteers the following week, his mother cut her hair so that she looked as though she were wearing a black swim cap. She wore jeans and t-shirts, and she told people it was her duty to see about her parents' home and their hometown, maybe do some good down there. Teddy wondered what his mother could possibly do that Catch could not.

The night before his mother left, Teddy's grandmother sat at the dining room table, her blue-gray hair dull now and shaggy. His grandmother looked tired as she held out a big set of keys for his mother, explaining which key went to which door and where to find everything like the silver, the china, the paintings, and the photographs.

His grandfather came and sat too, then placed a gun there on the glass table. Teddy had never seen a gun up close before, but this one with the wooden handle looked like something a pirate would have used.

His mother carefully picked up the gun with a paper napkin, and took it back to her room to pack in her bag along with bandages, rubbing alcohol, breathing masks, trail mix and other supplies. Teddy had seen the TV news about all the survivors with guns down there. People shot at each other for ice. He couldn't help but wonder and worry. Did his mother know how to wrap a wound? Did she know how to shoot?

After his mother left, Teddy went to school every day. Then, with his grandparents, he watched New Orleans unravel nightly on the TV news. His mother was gone three days before she called. Nothing, not even the cell phones, were working. Getting fuel was a problem too. When at last she came back safe after a week, carrying only a few silver pieces and some forks and knives in a damp, dirty Choctaw basket, she was quiet and pale. She said she needed a long hot shower and a good meal.

They gathered together in the living room, a formal, carpeted, all-beige room Teddy and his mother hardly ever used. His mother gave Teddy's grandfather the gun and his grandmother the keys. She needed neither, she said, because everything, including the doors, and mostly everybody was gone. "Just gone," she said again and again, her eyes welling up. "Nothing to open, no one to shoot." She told them as best she could about the miles of downed trees and flattened houses, and how the entire town was gone, really, and how stretches of their street were now torn up chunks of asphalt. She showed them dim, fuzzy pictures in her digital camera.

Teddy's mother was wrong. It wasn't all just gone. The pale yellow house was there, but just. It was a ruined, empty shell with no floors, no walls, no furniture and half a roof. In the camera, Teddy could only make out a lot of wood, dirt, mold and water. He couldn't recognize anything. One minute his mother couldn't speak, the next minute she shook, full of energy. He watched her and his grandparents cry, remembering their home, the pool, the rose garden, the badminton, the hydrangea bushes from the wedding, the beach, the shrimp boats, the pelicans, the neighbors.

It was hard for Teddy to picture the real hurricane, the one that was not the red and pink swirls on the TV weatherman's computer screen. He understood the water getting high and how it got inside the house, but he couldn't picture that water on his grandmother's light blue carpet or her things floating around, pushing themselves out into more water. He knew that while he sat at his desk at school, people like Catch had survived Katrina by being clever and getting to higher ground, but he also knew that people died, that the ropes broke loose at the harbor, and the boats had all floated away, some into the tops of trees where they were later found stuck. Now there were all those people down there, stuck too, eating Army food, then going to the bathroom in plastic bags.

Teddy's grandmother looked toward Teddy who was still trying to imagine the hurricane so that he could make himself cry along with the others. He was sad, he supposed, but he was not crying and he wondered if that was a problem. His grandmother wiped her face with a Kleenex and said, "Oh now, let's pull ourselves together. It was just a house. We're still here."

"But it's all gone," Teddy's mother repeated. "The house, the town, the church. The *credenza*, Momma. All your beautiful furniture."

Teddy didn't understand why his mother was so upset with the loss of the old furniture. After every summer, Thanksgiving and Christmas vacation to Mississippi, she told Teddy on the plane how *relieved* she was to get back home to Chicago, and how *glad* she was that she married a man like his father who could take her to Chicago and away from her parents' ancient, mildewy place.

His grandmother got up and sat next to Teddy. She put her arm around his shoulders and pulled him close enough so that he could smell the sherry on her breath. His grandmother was old, but not old old. Not smelly old. She had a sturdier build then his mother and her skin smelled of soap and hand cream, not perfume. "We're all going to be fine."

Weeks after her trip to the Gulf coast, Teddy would often see his mother standing in the middle of a room, unable to recall what she had been doing. She seemed incapable of completing sentences. She couldn't focus. This was the word his grandmother used. *Focus.* Judging from his mother's bad photography, Teddy thought it was the correct word. Then his mother was gone first for one night, then two, then for a whole week, staying with a friend in Hyde Park, a smart man who taught Physics at "You of See."

The Saturday morning his mother left for her trip to Canada with her friend, who was in fact her new boyfriend, Teddy stood before her as she packed.

"Do you like him more then you liked Dad?"

His mother stopped packing, her hand still on top of the blue nightgown she only wore on special occasions like Christmas.

"Not more. I like him different."

Her eyes were the color of the nightgown and he wondered if she and this professor talked about quantum theories and black holes. Teddy did not know why his parents divorced. They had not gotten along but they were together, now they were no longer together. Before was before. Now was now. It was as basic as $3-1=2$. He just wanted to know what that one thing was that caused the togetherness to break, because he was sure that it—that one thing that added up to divorce—was something as concrete as the numerical equations he was learning in math.

When his mother came to kiss him, he waved her away because of her sour, coffee-breath and she laughed, kissing him again and again while he held his own breath, wondering if this lack of oxygen affected his brain. When his mother finally stopped trying to kiss him, she looked past him. It was not a look that Teddy knew. She was not focusing. She was not thinking of him. She got up and closed her suitcases.

Teddy's grandmother sorted laundry while trying to make up a poem about folding Teddy into her life. She tried to smile as she struggled through her made-up rhymes and asked what he would like for lunch.

"I'm not hungry."

"Oh fiddlesticks," she said, hugging him to her. "We'll make do."

After they saw Teddy's mother off, and she was gone, Teddy and his grandparents went out for steaks and *frites*, and afterwards stopped at a drugstore to buy brand new toothbrushes.

For a while then everything was perfect.

Teddy and his grandmother went everywhere together. Teddy showed her where bloody battles had been fought along Dearborn. He told her how they were sitting on one of the great divides, one of the continental divides. She took him to the symphony, where he listened to the music while staring at the rows and rows of different colored hair on the pale necks in front of them. At intermission, they drank root beers and she showed him the Cha-cha-cha and the Charleston, then when everyone stopped looking, she said she thought they should both learn to play the violin.

Nastasia lived in their building, right down the hall from them, except that she had no view of the lake. She was tall, thin, and Russian with bangs and a fat cat. For the first month, Teddy and his grandmother held cigar boxes under their chins because Nastasia said they had to make ready to play. The day they finally played, Nastasia's cat began to weave in and out of their legs as they stood and plucked at the strings, single notes that even Teddy recognized as "Twinkle Twinkle Little Star." After the humiliation of the cigar boxes, Teddy thought this was everything now—to holding the violin tucked just so beneath his chin, and even though they were using their fingers and not the bow, he could hear a song, *the* song they were taught to play.

At the end of their thirty minutes, Teddy's grandmother put down her violin, found her wallet from her purse and counted out the cash while Nastasia scribbled something unreadable on the tops of their sheet music, nodding toward the bowl of Dum-Dums on her file cabinet, saying to Teddy what she always said in her low Russian accent, "Take candy."

Back home, at their place down the hall, the night they had learned "Twinkle Twinkle," the living room smelled of something alcoholic, and his grandfather was asleep in the green chair in front of the TV news, his newspapers all around him. The President was standing in front of a lit-up blueish Jackson Square in New Orleans.

"He doesn't deserve to be standing there," his grandmother whispered, bending to straighten the newspapers, and when she and Teddy both saw the gun on the floor, she quickly wrapped it with the papers, then told Teddy to go do his homework. He went to his room, glancing back to see his grandmother reappear without the gun, the walls flashing with the light of the TV screen.

That year, his fifth-grade year, Teddy's classroom smelled of pencil shavings, not crayons. He sat behind a new girl named Amy who wore her long brown hair in a ponytail that trailed onto the surface of his desk. He would, at times, color the ends of her hair with a yellow highlighter.

At his desk he read: *finding the square root of a number is the inverse operation of squaring that number. The square root of a number is that number times itself. Square roots of objects other than numbers can also be defined.*

Teddy worked his worksheet, then got up and stood before his teacher sitting at her desk. He gave her the worksheet. Slow-moving wasps crawled around the tips of the pens and pencils in a jar. Teddy knew his teacher didn't much care for him. He overheard her once say to another teacher in the teacher's lounge that she wondered if he—if Teddy was borderline autistic because he barely showed any emotion, that he was a just-the-facts kind of boy, and would never be able to read between the lines of anything.

"Just ignore them," his teacher said of the wasps, looking up from her grade book, stuffing a Kleenex inside the sleeve of her sweater. His teacher always had a cold.

Amy looked up as Teddy passed her desk. She was not yet halfway through her own worksheet on division.

"I like your braces," she said.

He ran his tongue across his front teeth. "Yeah?"

She nodded, and as he sat back down, he couldn't help but touch the tips of her hair.

He opened the same book he checked out of the school library once a week, the newest edition of Robert Ripley's *Believe It or Not*. He stared at the picture of the Wyandotte chicken that had survived thirty days without its head, only to choke to death on a corn kernel in an Arizona motel. It was a mystery to Teddy and also grotesque and he hoped it was alright that he stared and stared the way he did at all the pictures of other unexpected grotesques like the most pierced man, Luis Aguero, with 230 piercings on his body and head. The pictures in the book made him both delighted and off-balanced. He felt badly for staring, and even vaguely nauseated by what he saw, but he could not help but look and then look some more. It thrilled him to see and to know that such things, such events, such people and animals existed. It made him think of unexplainable possibilities.

In fifth grade, recess was called gym, and afterwards, at lunch, Amy sat down next to him and whispered, "Where's the state of emergency?" She said that she had heard that Teddy's grandparents had come up from Mississippi after the hurricane, and in the news, she kept hearing about this state of emergency. Teddy explained as best he could, and afterwards, Amy reached under the table and put her hand on his knee, telling him that her parents had made a significant donation to the Red Cross. Teddy was not sure what to say, and he could not think clearly with her hand there on his leg.

"Thank you," he said.

Teddy and his grandparents ate breakfast and dinner together and his grandfather had to have his bread on a bread plate, which his grandmother provided, and there most certainly had to be meat of some sort, not mixed or cooked up into anything with rice or nuts or dried fruit, just meat which his grandmother said was easy enough. Teddy was in charge of putting together the salad, which he kept adding to—raisins, pumpkin seeds—until at last his grandfather told him to quit messing with the lettuce.

His grandfather said next to nothing as they ate, and his grandmother touched his grandfather's hand frequently.

After four weeks, when his mother still had not come home, Teddy grew afraid of the dark in his room, especially the dark in his closet. His grandmother said nothing about this, and always at night, after dinner, accompanied him to bed, humming whatever song they had just learned from Nastasia.

He had a good idea of what his father would have said to all this business with the dark. *Nonsense*. His father believed in money and electronics. His father had not called since his mother had left for Canada.

One night Teddy came up with the idea of calling each of his parents on the phone, and then when their machines played, because they never ever answered their phones, Teddy and his grandmother would play a song on their violins, leaving the recordings on their voicemail.

He and his grandmother did this only when they had a new song to play, and that night, they played "Swallowtail Jig." They called his father first, leaving the song on the machine. Then after Teddy hung up, he dialed his mother's cell phone, knowing that the tune and the notes would give him something to think about when his grandmother eventually turned off his bedroom light.

But his mother interrupted their play by actually answering her phone. She said *Hi* to Teddy and he was not sure if her voice wavered because of her mood or their uncertain connection. She complimented him on his musical ability. He told her briefly about school and that he was getting really good at math and he knew this because it was not difficult for him, not like it was for the others in his class. She asked to speak with Teddy's grandmother.

Teddy watched his grandmother hold the phone to her ear, nodding her head, touching the ugly cactus that had not grown one inch in four years in its plastic pot on his bureau. She walked the room, picking up books and clothes he'd left on the floor, twirling the globe round once, then rattling the little jar half filled with Teddy's baby teeth. She'd had her hair

ırker at some salon on Michigan Avenue and she
ʼe like his mother used to look.

..ᴄn she hung up, Teddy asked his grandmother what
his mother had said. She told him his mother would be a little
while longer in Canada.

"How much longer?"

His grandmother pulled the sheets up to his chin, then
kissed the top of his head as though he was still just a boy and
not ten years old. "I can't rightly tell. But we'll make do." She
sounded so southern then.

That night Teddy overheard his grandparents talking in
their guest room. His grandfather was saying that he'd had
enough of their daughter, that all her life they'd worried about
her even though they'd done everything for her, sent her to
private schools, Sunday school, bought her nice clothes, and
now here she was, a divorcee, running around Canada with an
academic commie named Ivan.

"Ivan the Terrible," his grandfather said.

"She's forty-nine," his grandmother sighed. "She's just
going through something."

"She's a grown woman with a child. We've got our
own worries."

His grandmother picked Teddy up after school in a cab
the following day, then they headed for The Art Institute
where she said she needed to find a statue so that she could
sit and look at it. In Gallery 271, they settled on a bench in
front of Ceres, the Roman goddess of grain.

"She doesn't have a face," Teddy said.

"Probably just as well," his grandmother said, slipping off
her shoes. She was tired. Teddy had overheard her say to his
grandfather that morning that she didn't want to hear anymore
about insurance companies, flood, wind, or mold damage. She
didn't want to talk about *that house* anymore. She had said *that
house* as though it was any house, and not their yellow home in
front of the Gulf, in the town, the place they had loved.

She read out the information from the plaque. The Art Deco sculpture was the model for the big one on top of the Board of Trade building.

"That's where Dad used to work," Teddy said.

"She's the patron saint of traders," his grandmother said, pointing to the sheaf of wheat in Ceres' hand, which had no fingers, just lines suggesting them. "The wheat has more detail then she does."

His grandmother sighed and said that Ceres was a disappointment, more silver column than woman. While she talked, she rubbed perfume on her wrists from a free trial bottle, then straightened the scarf around her neck. His grandmother wore the one good scarf she came to Chicago with when they went out. It was a silky blue, the color of her eyes, with yellow flowers and a border that looked like rain. She said that Ceres' straight back and her hair up in a bun like that made her look more British than Roman. Too slick and devoid of emotion, she said, sounding tired and sad.

"The Romans called her Ceres. The Greeks called her Demeter. Her daughter, Persephone, disappeared one day while gathering flowers. Suddenly the ground split open and Hades came with dark horses and captured her, plunging them both back into the ground where he had an underground palace. He sat her on a throne of black marble, decked her out in gold and precious stones, then offered her a pomegranate. He was a good host. At first she refused to eat, but what can I say? She got hungry. She ate the fruit of the dead. Big mistake. Meanwhile on earth, the willows wept and there were no more flowers or fruit because her mother, Ceres, was so distraught."

"So that's our winter?"

She hugged him. "Such a brilliant boy. I do like to watch you think."

"But it's just a story."

"Makes all the sense in the world to me. Ceres cuts a deal with Zeus, Persophone's dad. He said Persophone had to live with Hades for one month for each pomegranate seed she had eaten. Then she could come back up to earth. When mother and daughter were together, the earth was warm and bore fruit."

"Grandmother?" He knew what he had to say would be a disappointment. He did not want to appear shallow or stupid, but his head ached.

"I'm hungry."

She laughed and said that he was wonderful. "Oh you're so brilliant and interesting and wonderful," she said, saying his name in the nicest way, and he knew then that if this was true what she said, if he really was brilliant and interesting and wonderful, then she was too, but more so because she was his grandmother, the root of their square.

They went to a café across the street and his eyes watered from walking into the cold wind. His grandmother asked the waiter to turn off the TV news about FEMA and they talked about how his parents had met at a party. "It was hard knowing my only daughter was going to move to Chicago, but he was considered a catch," she said of his father. "He was a good provider." She told Teddy about the wedding parties she called showers they had all along the Mississippi Gulf Coast and into New Orleans. His grandmother appeared happy to remember the house as it once was and herself as a younger woman and Teddy was happy to know more about his parents. Neither one of them mentioned the divorce.

"I know I shouldn't ask, but do you have a girlfriend?" his grandmother said, cutting away the bitten parts on her scone. She wrapped the rest of the scone in a napkin. She would carry the scone back to Teddy's grandfather who would still be seated in the big green chair, staring at all that bad television news about the war and the hurricane both.

"My friend does. He thinks she maybe doesn't like him because he's kind of a nerd. He asked me what he should do about it though."

"Well, he could be just exceptionally nice to her. Maybe bring her a small gift."

His grandmother shrugged, putting the scone into her purse. Outside their window, Teddy could see the wind freezing puddles of water into alligator shapes on the street.

They quickly advanced to "Harvest Home." They used their bows now too, and one day Nastasia picked up her violin and played with them. She played full chords. How could he not notice the difference? When would they be able to learn to play like that? When would she teach them how to shake their fingers too? Hearing Nastasia play, more than anything, Teddy wanted it all right then, not just this song, but the shaking, the full sound, the wholer song.

Nastasia stopped playing to line up his fingers, which she called his animals.

"They are not in their pens. What happened to doggy? He's going into Kitty's yard. Animals, they are stupid. You in charge. Be angry with animals. You must discipline. You must be strict so they get as smart as you."

Teddy put down his violin. "When can we learn a real song? Like the ones you play."

Nastasia looked at him, then at his grandmother who only shrugged.

"There is the Christmas concert," Nastasia started, flipping through the sheet music on their stands, passing the baby stuff with all the elaborate cats and dogs she'd drawn with colored pencils. She stopped at one page then played the first few stanzas. His grandmother inhaled.

"That's what they played at my daughter's wedding at our home in Mississippi. "She read the title on the page." But I thought it was Vivaldi's 'Spring.'" She sounded young again. Happy.

"Ha!" Nastasia said, picking up their bows. "No no, it's Pachelbel's Canon in D. Slow and beautiful, but just say *piece of cake*, then it will be easy and your mind will follow and all your animals will stay in yards." Nastasia showed them how to better hold the bow with the pinky just so. She called the pinky a rabbit and told them not to kill their rabbits.

"OK? Nobody dead? Animals well behaved? You strong? Be bright. Be brave. Be expressive."

Nastasia had them hold their violins to their chins, bows in place while she counted in Russian. Teddy stood up straight beside his grandmother. They both smiled at one another as if they knew a secret. He could have stood beside his grandmother like that for a lifetime.

Then all at once everything changed.

Teddy and his grandmother had finished practicing their canon one night, reminding each other to *keep their animals loosen*. They laughed in the kitchen preparing dinner, imitating Nastasia's Russian accent. "Don't play into your stomach," his grandmother said. "Keep beautiful."

"Be bright, be brave, be expressive," he said. "Take candy."

Teddy's grandfather was on the phone with the insurance company, his face reddening as he listened. Fighting with the insurance company was his new full-time job. That's what Teddy's grandmother said. His grandfather had even laughed when she said this, and he had said, "What else am I gonna do with all this time but argue with them on whether or not this was wind or water damage?"

"We have to make a decision," Teddy's grandfather said. His hair looked to be getting whiter. "Sell or rebuild."

"Holey moley," his grandmother said. Teddy put Vivaldi's *Four Seasons* on the CD player. "Spring" was playing. "Do we really have to decide that now?"

After dinner, his grandmother said she was tired. The day and all this talk of hurricane damage gave her pain that ran across her back. His grandfather looked at her then and said her color was off. He offered to call their doctor, but he wasn't sure if he was in Texas now or Louisiana. Teddy walked with her to the guestroom.

"There aren't many birds here in the city, are there?" his grandmother said, sitting there on the edge of the bed. They could hear the strong, cold wind outside coming off the lake, whistling through the windows. "You know my brother, your great uncle helped build the sea wall along the Mississippi gulf coast at the beginning of the century. Every house in Pass Christian had its own pier back then. You could fish at the end and catch crabs. Everything I loved was down there."

Teddy looked at her, knowing how much she must be missing her home. She was inside here, when he knew she should have been outside there, in Mississippi, walking the porch before she slept, the way she liked. Once, at a shrimp boil on the beach at the Fourth of July bonfire, she taught him how to light up the end of a stick, and with the sparks, they wrote their names in the air, that and *hello*. He had only been five or six then, and when they looked up at the night sky, he had said *communicating* which made her laugh.

"I'm sorry you lost your house," he said.

"You're an angel is what you are," she said, motioning him to her, hugging him close and tight. "My perfect angel."

He flapped his hands like wings and tried to make her laugh.

"Don't be stiffy," he said with his Russian accent.

He was still asleep when they came all at once at dawn, rolling his grandmother out to the hall on a gurney and then into the elevator, down to the lobby, and into an ambulance, which he could not ride. He and his grandfather followed in a cab.

At the hospital, the doctor, a squat man with brown eyes, came out too quickly from the emergency room. He said she died—he said that word, *died*—of heart failure, the sort of thing that so often goes undetected in women her age.

Without thinking, Teddy brought his grandfather's hand to his lips and kissed the tips of his grandfather's fingers. His grandfather only stared at the doctor who continued to say things they did not hear. Teddy looked at the linoleum floor, then at the pay phone down the hall.

When they went back to the apartment, Teddy couldn't make sense of anything. All the rooms still smelled of the chicken dinner he and his grandmother cooked the night before. He was cold, and he allowed his teeth to rattle.

Then his mother came home, and when Teddy saw her at the door with her suitcases, he saw a woman, not his mother. Her hair had grown out so that the salt and pepper sides blew back like feathers. She looked less thin, sturdier. He saw not *Mom* then but Dianne, and for a moment he realized she would never be able to talk with him, not in the way his grandmother had. She would only be Dianne. He understood this and he pushed this new knowledge of his mother into the back of his mind, so that later, he would re-examine it in his room, alone, and figure out what to do about it.

She stepped forward, stopped, then reached into her purse and gave him a piece of chocolate which, when he opened it later, was old and gray. He hugged her, then stepped back to let her in, as though they were on a date and it was his apartment.

"I know I shouldn't be hungry, but I am." She was using the voice she used when she spoke to him in front of other people. "Is it asking too much for someone to pour me a Scotch?"

His mother was on the phone most of the time, making so many arrangements, telling people, sharing her worries about her father. It wasn't supposed to happen. For days she said so. This wasn't supposed to happen. Teddy's grandmother was supposed to be the one who lived on and on, in her house, on the coast. Teddy's grandfather mostly stayed in the guest room and said nothing.

One morning, while Teddy and his grandfather ate cereal, Teddy's mother hung up the phone and announced to them that they could not bury Teddy's grandmother in Pass Christian, Mississippi—the hurricane had demolished the cemetery and they were having enough trouble with the bodies that had already been buried there. The water had pushed up caskets into the streets.

The hurricane had gone and washed through his grandparents' home and now it felt as though it was washing through their lives again. This storm had grabbed hold of them and wouldn't let go.

"Did you call Catch?" Teddy asked. "Maybe he could do something. *You* should call him, Grandfather."

His grandfather looked at Teddy and for a clear-eyed moment Teddy felt they had an understanding.

"Hand me the phone," his grandfather said, the first words he spoke in days. As he dialed, his mother slipped away and into the guest room. She came out holding something solid wrapped in a newspaper, and Teddy guessed it was the gun.

His grandfather's shoulders shook as he tried to speak into the phone. Then his grandfather said *I can't* and handed Teddy the phone. Teddy listened, not to what Catch was saying, but to the slow, gravely voice he knew.

In his mind, Teddy practiced saying it. And then he heard his own voice saying it out loud. *My grandmother's dead.* He swallowed. He thought he might throw up. He didn't want to say it or think it again. Ever.

Again, Teddy listened to Catch's slow voice. Again, he didn't hear the words, but he sat down near his grandfather, carefully listening to the sound of the voice on the other end of the line. It was hard to move his legs or his arms.

The night before the funeral, Teddy sat up in his bed and put in front of him a book with a cloaked figure on the cover. He could not make sense of the words. He closed the book and looked out the window at the sky and a rooftop. He pretended that there was a bare tree there, with a bird on the branch, and he pretended that the bird was his pet and that the bird could understand everything he said and thought.

When his mother came to kiss him goodnight, he didn't wave her away.

"You're not going to marry him, are you?" he asked her.

"Oh God. I don't know, Teddy." She sat on the edge of his bed making him roll closer. They stayed that way, without saying anything.

"Let's just get through this, OK?" his mother said.

The cab driver steered with his wrist while he drove them to the visitation. In the backseat of the cab he sat between his grandfather and his mother who kept pulling Teddy close, and asking him if he was all right. Even though it was snowing, Teddy reached over and put the windows down to feel the cold air. He needed to feel. That morning he had practiced looking sad and solemn in front of the mirror as he tied his tie the way his father had taught him. He knew he was acting, but he did not know what else to do. He waited patiently for a feeling of sadness to overwhelm him so that he could cry, but nothing came.

It was full winter. The trees were black, naked limbs and now the snow was wrapping them up in white blankets. On his black glove, the snowflakes were all different up close, each one wonderful. He knew that if he continued to look out the window and examine snowflakes, his mother would stop asking him questions.

He crossed and re-crossed himself. He buttoned and unbuttoned his good jacket. He stood before the open casket where his grandmother lay with her sprayed hair and her pinkened arms. He wanted to reach over and brush away the powder from her face. He was glad his mother had thought to put the blue scarf around her neck, the way she liked it tied when she was about to set out on a new cultural adventure. He stayed there before her. If he stayed there long enough, she would open her eyes, turn to him and tell him again what a brilliant boy he was, her perfect angel. He stood and waited for this.

He heard someone say that it was a good, solid coffin. That it looked as though it had been made to fit her. He overheard an old man say, "I consider her death hurricane damage. Katrina is still killing. She's part of the aftermath."

Teddy considered this word *aftermath*. His grandmother was after math. 2-1=1. His grandmother had been so much like him, but older. They were each other times two.

Teddy tipped back and forth on his heels when he spoke with any of the adults, thanking them when they put dollar bills into his coat jacket, smiling politely when they complimented him on his behavior. He knew they liked children to be quiet. He had nothing to say to them anyway.

His mother introduced him to her smart boyfriend who was really a man named Ivan with bushy eyebrows who called himself an astrophysicist. He told Teddy that he had a dog named Syntax whom he thought Teddy would like. Teddy's father would have made fun of the eyebrows. Teddy missed his father. His father could not make it to the funeral and it was as though he were avoiding another holiday.

"Let's make a deal," the astrophysicist said. "Whatever you can't Google, you can ask me."

Outside snow was falling. Christmas was coming. His grandmother was not there to ask him what he would like. She would not be there when he turned twelve or even twenty. There would be no more cards. Teddy did not know what to make of any of it. To Teddy it had seemed all of them would go on living as they had been living, and their house would always be there, anchored in a town that never aged, and his grandmother would go on forever, watching him go on forever. He had assumed this.

The term from Teddy's math book, *Place Value,* came to mind. In the decimal system, the value of a digit depends on its place. If they were the digits, then they would be changed now because their place and so much of what they had been was destroyed.

His mother led him to a kitchen in the back of the funeral home where there were sandwiches made with wet turkey. His mother fixed him a plate, but he could not eat. He only poked at the food. There were other children there for another funeral. They sat on the floor eating jellybeans and chips. He did and did not want to join them. When they visited, his grandmother used to play with him on the floor of her living room on the coast in Mississippi, after they had played in the sand on the beach in front of their house, the house that had drowned. She had shown him his first blue heron on that beach. On the floor of her living room on the coast, she never said *Not now, honey* and they built buildings with Legos, put puzzles of fish together, rolled cars, and made windmills from Tinker Toy sticks.

The other funeral at the funeral home was for a child. There were colored balloons instead of flowers and long lines of people with their own, living children coming in from the cold. To Teddy, it somehow made sense that there was a child in a coffin and his grandmother in another and that they were in the same funeral home. Teddy knew that his grandmother would help the child find her way. His grandmother was like that. In his mind, Teddy could see his grandmother taking the girl's hand, stopping traffic to cross a street hanging on a cloud made of spun sugar. The child and his grandmother would sing a song they had learned from Nastasia. *Grasshopper grasshopper*, they would sing. His grandmother would teach the girl. His grandmother would enjoy watching the girl think. For that moment, Teddy wished he were the dead girl.

His mother had asked him to bring along a book because she said it would be a long day. Teddy found his Ripley's *Believe It or Not*, brought it to a table and sat down, opening the book to a picture of the smallest waist on a living person, Cathie Jung Usa, who at 5 foot 8 inches tall had a 15-inch waist. Teddy turned back to the page with the longest surviving headless chicken named Mike. Mike's owner, Lloyd Olsen, fed and watered the headless chicken directly into his gullet with an eyedropper. Teddy stared at the words that made the story that continued to defy logic. There was no mention of Katrina in Ripley's. Maybe the hurricane would make it into the next edition. Maybe not. Anything was possible.

Sitting there in the kitchen at the funeral home, Teddy looked up from his *Believe It or Not* and he saw the girl he knew to be Amy. She wore her hair down and pushed back behind her ears. She walked straight toward him, then stopped and said, "I'm so sorry about your grandmother." Her eyes were a watery light blue.

His throat tightened and his eyes were stinging, and as he stood up, his chair fell back and he didn't bother to right it. He took one step toward her—it only took one step—and he put his arms around her and he breathed in her orange candy smell as he held her so close that his lips touched the soft hairs at the nape of her neck.

That night Teddy dreamed brown-black, dirty water flooded his grandmother's room and she could not swim and she could not breath from her bed and there were floating coffins all around and he woke up panting. In the dark, Teddy got up and he went to his mother who woke up halfway. She did not tell him to be a big boy and go back to his own bed, but instead, she lifted the covers. He climbed in, warming his feet between her feet, his face near her hands, and then he listened to her breath fall into a whisper.

In the moonlight, he could see the firecracker lines left over from when her eyes closed up when she smiled. Through the wall, he could hear his grandfather snoring.

There had not been time for him to write or draw a get-well card for his grandmother because she had not been sick. He should have helped out more, cooked the meat for his grandfather, fetched the bread and butter plates, filled the water glasses. He wished he had recognized their time together more clearly, said something about it to her, but then, that would have taken something out of it too.

During mass the following day, the elderly priest could not find his place in the Bible. He looked the way his father used to look when he couldn't find his tax records. The priest who no longer looked like a priest, but rather like a scared man in a bathrobe, flipped through the Bible in front of him. No one said anything. They could all hear the splutter of candles. Finally, they watched as the priest carefully read through what looked to be the Table of Contents until at last he found what he was looking for, smiled, flipped to the page, looked up, nodded, and began speaking in his priest voice, using his priest face, looking like a priest again.

When it was his turn, Teddy stood up and went to the alter himself where he played from memory Pachelbel's Canon in D which his grandmother had thought was Vivaldi. He made every attempt to play bright and brave. His fingers were not stiffy and all through the allegro, he made his animals behave and the cat and the dog stayed in their own yards and he was able to shake his fingers just so to make the notes come out loud and clear and strong. He did not look up from his violin when he heard people sniffing. He stayed focused.

After the mass and after the funeral, and finally after the long luncheon, they stayed at the banquet hall near the forest preserve next to the cemetery where they laid his grandmother into the dark hole, and buried her in the frozen ground. He could not stop thinking of her there, inside that cold hole. He hoped she would meet up with a good host. She deserved an underground palace, too, one with a throne of black marble like Cere's daughter had.

It had stopped snowing and the night was lit up with all the white. Inside, his grandfather and his mother stayed seated at the big table as the others left. They ordered themselves another drink and discussed how much everything cost. Their voices grew louder.

Teddy went outside alone, past the parking lot, toward the edge of the woods. He began to hum the real Vivaldi concerto softly to himself. He found a patch of unbroken snow. He turned around careful to stay in his own footprints, then crouched and slowly sat back. He lay down flat and fit his body into the snow, snugly, the snow crunching as he did this. They had buried his grandmother that day and he had held Amy the day before, and he had no one to tell, but he recognized that it still happened. He lay there. He closed his eyes and concentrated, humming the concerto louder now, as he moved his arms up and down, his legs out and back. He stopped moving and he stopped humming too, and for a soft moment, he stayed like that, thinking on the notes of "Spring." Keeping his eyes closed, he stood without using his hands, taking time to get his balance. Then he opened his eyes wide to behold his offering.

MONT ROYAL

The dinner was in the old part of Montreal where Diane could hear horses and carriages on the brick streets. The hostess lived alone in a home a furrier built in the early 1800s, the stone walls and the beams stripped now and exposed. When she and Ivan walked into the living room, everything was bathed in burgundy light, with a fire going in the big hearth, and she could smell meat and potatoes roasting in the oven.

Ivan was in town for a physics conference, and while there he wanted Diane to meet his son, Darko, which they had done earlier that day. Ivan was better dressed than most academics, because he was European. He was a tall man with graying hair, dark eyes and a beautiful Slavic accent that transformed her name into something sweet and edible. Diane wore a slim, black dress with kitten-heeled pumps, and she had put her hair up in a snood. Ivan smiled every time he looked at her from across the room.

Over the rich dinner, Diane sat beside the hostess, a clothing designer named Cassandra with curly red hair. She wore a green strapless dress, highlighting her muscular neck and shoulders. Cassandra told Diane she was from Alberta. She had just come back from Mongolia, and she had swiped her designing ideas that season from Mongolian armor. "I was in the museums there, and it suddenly occurred to me. Put two spaghetti straps on all that hammered gold, and boom, you've got a summer shift," she said.

When the torte came drizzled with white chocolate, Diane was drunk enough to tell Cassandra all her woes about the Mississippi Gulf Coast which had been destroyed by the hurricane. "When you see the chaos up-close, when you see homes and gardens blown apart like that," Diane said, dizzy with the thought, "it just leaves you breathless. Who knows when something can just blow us all away?"

Even though she spent her growing-up years in Lubbock, Diane rarely told people she was from Texas. She had spent the best summers of her life vacationing or living on the coast of Mississippi with her parents, friends, and later, her ex-husband, and the watery shell and shrimp memories were so strong, she felt she was more from there, born of the Sound, straight into the sand.

Just before hurricane season, she had put a down payment on the Gulf coast property next to her parents' home. She hadn't told anybody this, not even her ex-husband. It was to be a surprise, a gift to her parents, her son, herself. Selling the Chicago condo with all the memories of her first bad marriage and moving down there to Pass Christian, Mississippi, was going to be her second chance to become a better mother, a better daughter, a happier person. But then, in Chicago, when her son Teddy showed her a satellite picture of the hurricane in the paper, she could only stare speechless at the giant destructive gyre of storm clouds swirling around the Gulf of Mexico.

"Is Diane telling you that her beloved town of Pass Christian is gone?" Ivan asked, standing behind Cassandra. He felt comfortable enough in this woman's home to pour wine for the guests. "My own country disappeared to become Serbia and Montenegro. We are both now orphans, made for each other." He kissed Diane on the back of her neck and moved to pour for the next guest.

"I can't help but envy your pain," Cassandra said. "Ivan lost his childhood home too. This is what first drew me to him."

Diane smeared the white chocolate drizzle around and took a bite of cake. She was drinking and crying too much lately, comforting herself with too many sweets.

Whenever Diane spoke of the hurricane, she realized how wrong it all came out. It hadn't been The Katrina War. This was a natural disaster with a woman's name and slow government response. Get over it, she told herself over and over. For a while she even felt important, caught up in such a newsworthy event. When "her hurricane" made the covers of magazines, she felt as though she had made the covers. For a while, she couldn't stop talking about the destruction and the debris she had seen. After the storm, the coast really did look like those old images of Hiroshima after the bomb, and she really had been in danger when she went down there. But back in Chicago, while her friends moved on to talk about charity auctions, ski vacations, and the Middle East, Diane's mind was still fixed on the unmoving pile of rubble that was once her paradise.

"Very compelling," Cassandra said, looking at Diane's scrawny shoulders and arms. "My work needs more suffering. All those things in the hurricane washed and made different now, they'll have a Katrina patina, like you."

Diane sniffed and stared at Cassandra.

"It's clever, isn't it." She brushed aside some of the red hair that had uncoiled down her forehead. "I'll have to use that somehow."

Diane's cell phone rang inside her purse. She recognized her mother's number and turned off the ringer. The rest of the table was complaining about the Bushes and the prime minister. Someone tried to recall something Khrushchev once said.

"Now there was a memorable tyrant," Ivan said, making them all laugh.

They were a mix of academics and artists—a gathering that shrank as the evening went on, evolving into a drunken, morose circle in the end. When he left Yugoslavia after the conflict, Ivan had attained Canadian citizenship, then later landed his faculty position at the University of Chicago. He traveled to Montreal at least four times a year to visit his friends and his son, who was in his last year at McGill. Diane wondered why Ivan made such a big deal out of Montreal. Sure, there were the great restaurants and the tiny museums with OK paintings of ice cutters, people gathering seaweed, and early settlers being attacked by wolves, but really, why keep coming back?

After too much wine, Cassandra kept saying *fucked up* so frequently Diane began to feel dizzy and unable to hear anything correctly. She thought one man said *insulting* instead of *consulting* financial services. She was ready to go, but Ivan was not. She reminded him they had to get up early, that she was to meet up with Darko for tennis.

"My name has nothing to do with being dark," Darko had said to Diane over lunch that afternoon. "It's a derivative from the Slavic *dar*, meaning gift." He had smiled when he said the word *gift*. He was lovely and tall with brown eyes and long ears, like his father's.

At lunch, Ivan was consumed by an argument he'd had with his departmental chair before he and Diane left Chicago. His chair wanted Ivan to slow down with his scholarly work and focus more on his teaching. "Can you imagine?" Ivan had said, unable to touch his sandwich. "He could have another Nobel on his faculty."

"Maybe your students miss you, Dad."

Ivan said something in Slavic to Darko, and then he said something in French. The three grew quiet as they sipped coffee. Diane and Ivan had agreed that they both needed a certain amount of freedom. She had also learned not to say just anything that occurred to her. Ivan sometimes said she sounded like one of his students, which really meant one of the students he did not prefer. He was careful never to say that he hated his students and teaching. Diane knew that Ivan was grateful for teaching because it allowed him to live and conduct his research in the United States.

"*Ce n'est pas la meme chose*," Ivan said to his son. It was the only thing Diane understood. *It's not the same thing*.

After he had his final drink, Ivan finally took Diane back to the apartment. She listened to her messages. Her mother and Teddy had called. They were learning the violin together and had taken to calling and leaving songs on her voicemail, short ditties that made her feel sad and guilty.

After the hurricane destroyed her parents' home, Diane asked them to come to Chicago to live with her and Teddy. When they came, Diane left, first to go to Mississippi for two weeks to see what was left of her property, and then to perhaps salvage what she could from her parents' home. When she saw her son's first bed, the wrought iron twisted and mangled in the branches of a live oak, she couldn't stop crying. The house she had bought was gone. And the water had hollowed out her parents' house, the walls barely standing. The furniture that had so many intimate associations and confidential histories, all of it was either gone or destroyed, and with these things, it felt as though both her past and future were wiped out as well.

When Diane returned to Chicago, she spent most all her time with Ivan, at his place on 59th, where his bedroom window looked out onto the roof of the Museum of Science and Industry, its dome a breast, the building itself a relic of the 1893 World Columbian Exposition.

Then Diane left again, this time with Ivan to another country. Her parents could look after Teddy. He was in the fifth grade now, a big boy. She begged her mother to understand. Her mother had asked only, "Why?" and "Are you sure about him?" then finally she nodded and suggested that Diane bring some nice perfume and a scarf.

At last Diane and Ivan were together again in bed. While they were in Montreal, they stayed in Ivan's spare, black and white, brushed stainless steel one-bedroom apartment that he sublet during the peak seasons. It was September, off-season in Montreal, still hurricane season on the coast.

"Tell me formulas," she said, stifling a hiccup. He laughed, but he began to recite as though the numbers, quotients, fractions, sines and cosines were lines of poetry. Tipsy but sure of himself, he whispered to Diane about her delta, the alluvial Delta of the south, and his mathematical delta, a variable, a function, a finite increment.

"Nothing," Ivan murmured, kissing her neck and her breasts. "No levees can hold me back."

When he was on top of her, his whole mouth covered hers, and she felt as though he were filling her back up with air. She was a punctured beach ball and now he was springing her back to life again to become mobile, airborne even, and elevated. Buoyed by Ivan, she floated.

While Ivan delivered his paper on the Non-Abelian tensor product of two Engel groups of rank "n," Diane and Darko played tennis at Jarry Park. It was an unusually warm fall and they played outside in sweatshirts and shorts on clay courts and the green sand stuck to the backs of their legs. Diane had not played in years, but she was still in shape from all the swimming, and whatever ball she couldn't hit, she at least chased down, sliding across the clay, making Darko laugh.

She was the first to ask to stop, thinking she might have an inner ear imbalance because again she felt light-headed and woozy. For a moment she thought of a FEMA tent she had seen on the coast. Outside the tent, a hand-lettered cardboard sign stayed propped on a rusty metal folding chair, reading *Free Medical, 9-5*. Darko fetched cold water and steered Diane to a nearby picnic bench inside a gazebo, and as she got her balance back, Darko talked about his studies with insects. The smell of spun sugar hung in the air.

"It's interesting that after all you and your father went through, neither one of you went into politics or even economics," she said.

"After all that we went through, there was no way in hell we were going into politics or economics. We saw politics lead to genocide and we saw that everybody, our leaders and their men, got away with murder." Diane watched five old men playing bocce and a young woman running her dogs.

"I started with water mites before I moved on to periodical cicadas," Darko said, leaning back on the picnic bench, crossing his legs at the ankles. "The broods that interest me most are in your American southern states."

They took the metro to the Botanical Gardens where there was an insectarium. They saw Mexican darkling beetles made into living jewelry, brooches called *Ma'Kech* that crawled around on gold leashes pinned to women's dresses, living sometimes up to eighteen months. They saw a necklace made out of green beetles, all of them dead, and stag and rhinoceros beetles turned into pets. Later, as they walked around the grounds outside, the beautiful gardens made Diane long for the coast house she'd hoped to live in all over again. She wrote down the names of her favorite blooming perennials using Darko's pen and paper: *Perovskia Russian sage, Delphinium belladonna, Aquilegia vulgaris in clementine blue*, and *Baptista starlite prairieblues*.

They had lunch in the Garden Restaurant and they each drank wine. She was on vacation, after all. She heard Christmas music somewhere, though it wasn't even Thanksgiving. Young people were climbing a fake wall nearby. The girls were rigged in rope climbing harnesses that reminded Diane of a scene from an old porn movie she had seen with her ex-husband.

Sitting across the table from her, Darko smelled of warm air and suntan lotion, nothing like Ivan. She missed being near the water. She was happiest around water.

When her cell phone rang, Darko ordered more wine. Diane listened to the violin jig on the other end of the line, and she broke in to interrupt the song.

"Teddy? Teddy? Is that you?" Diane smiled at Darko as she spoke to her son, listening to what he said about school, violin lessons, and math. She watched a little girl at another table stand up and press her face into her mother's hip. Teddy had never done anything like that. From the time he could walk, her son had always been able to stand alone. People told her this kind of independence was good. Diane impressed herself with her son's ability to cope so that she would feel less guilty about leaving him in Chicago with his homeless grandparents.

"Can I talk with your grandmother?"

Diane thought about her mother standing there reaching for the phone, her lavender blue, holier-than-thou eyes, telling her, but not saying, she was a terrible mother and daughter too, just as she had been a terrible wife. Diane had never been close to her mother because she felt she was nothing like her mother. Diane knew she was nothing but a disappointment, turning into this daughter with no career and now no husband.

"Hi, Mom?" Diane winked at Darko. He poured her wine.

"Diane." Her mother's voice sounded so far away. "What are you doing? You can't keep running away like this. Your father. He's not well, and you being away only makes him more upset."

"What's wrong with Dad?"

"He's just not himself. He sits in front of the television and watches all the awful news," her mother said. "And now he's worried about you."

"Mom, I'm fine. This is just what I needed. Really. Would you tell Dad that? I'm going to be staying here a while longer." She felt like she was sixteen again, asking to stay longer at the party. Diane could hear herself as she spoke, too, the slow drawl coming on.

Maybe here in Montreal, she was finally becoming a woman of the south again. The women she knew in Mississippi still used hair spray, still wore a lot of make up and dressed, really dressed, for everything, especially lunch. And yet, they never really did anything northerners considered valuable—they endured, plugged on, so why wasn't that enough? The night of the hurricane, one mother saved her baby boy by floating him in a Tupperware bowl. Another woman Diane knew survived three days on a bag of peeled shrimp she cooked outside on a hubcap. *So what* if there were no Marie Curies coming out of her home state, maybe there would be something else.

After the phone call, Diane had more wine and two slices of pie. She asked Darko about his girlfriends. He told amusing date stories, and then, he said, his last girlfriend asked him to piss on her, which he did, and which, he said, the girl had liked.

"No thank you," Diane said. "For future reference."

It was a term her ex-husband had used ages ago, when they had just finished making love on the beach in front of what she hoped would be her future home, not yet destroyed then, on the coast. He told her she should remember how much she liked doing it outdoors. She asked why. "For future reference," he had said, spoiling the moment, and now, all these years later, sitting with Darko in Montreal, Diane saw that her husband had been preparing her for their eventual divorce. They had married in a predictable way, after he'd earned his MBA, and they had both been so eager to register for the silver and china and stuff that would surely enable them to get on with the obvious, foreseeable success of their lives. But by saying *future reference*, wasn't he suggesting that he was not to be her future partner in some future sex on some future beach in his future life? Wasn't he thinking beyond her?

Darko sat now across the table from Diane, studying her, smiling, tracing the rim of his glass with his middle finger, trying to appear older than his years. Diane could tell he too was considering the future of her reference.

He was a beautiful young man, strong and healthy. She was forty-nine years old, flat chested, and lean. She managed her gray hair with frequent and regular hair colorings, and she still had all her parts, inside and out. She still wanted, and she wanted to see. She wanted to see if she could still get whatever she wanted.

Future reference? Why had she said this? It was wrong on so many levels.

She was setting herself up. She knew this, right then. Making her own bed. The awaiting catastrophe in her relationship with Ivan would be all her own doing. She had seen her own marriage crumble, her parents' home gone, and her future plans for a new life blown away. There she sat in another country without a plan, out of balance, off-center, and free to do as she pleased. Was this her way of seeing just how damaged she could get?

"Edward Wilson is speaking at the university," Darko said as they started back to the Metro. Her legs and back felt stiff from sitting so long. "He's the most amazing entomologist and chief bug man of all time. He's southern, too."

Darko put his arm around Diane's waist, resting his hand on her hipbone. The move made her feel young and slim. "Or we could just skip it," he said.

Ivan's paper was very well received. That night, over dinner, he told Diane that his colleagues from all over the globe toasted him at the reception, and later a renowned scholar asked if his university journal could publish the paper.

Diane held up her water glass. "To Ivan Banovic."

"Perhaps I should hold out for another offer, a better offer," he said, thinking into his glass.

"Best to take this one while you can," she said. Her words came out flat, but Ivan didn't seem to notice. He was going on now about the Engel group, explaining to her that a set can be numbers or letters with certain properties and that two Engel groups can have special properties. She stopped trying to understand.

She was tired and her head hurt from all the wine she and Darko had drunk that afternoon. At first it had been sweet and different. She called him baby and sugar and all the rest. Close your eyes, baby. Open your mouth, sugar. But then he rolled her around this way and that, using her as a prop for some movie playing in his mind. She supposed she should have expected this. He pressed hard into her and she disappeared, swallowed whole and still alive like Jonah inside the whale, except that afterwards, she felt as though she had been spat out, pissed upon, and altogether deflated.

It was the sweet love she missed most. And now she was getting along in years. That was what she felt most now, her age. Does all sweetness have to go away with age? Afterwards, lying in Darko's ridiculously narrow bed, she thought of the gem-colored leashed beetles she had seen that day, manacled, poked, threaded through, and made into accessories.

"Tomorrow I want to take you up Mont Royal," Ivan said. He was feeling strong and confidant, his English elegant and sure. "We'll have breakfast with Darko, then hike up."

"I think I'll skip breakfast," she said. Ivan tilted his head.

"I thought you liked Darko."

"I don't need to be eating so much." She smiled, patting her tummy.

"Then he and I will meet up alone."

"Good."

"Father and son."

"Yes." She took a deep breath, and decided to begin drinking again, after all. "I'll meet you at the foot and we can hike up together," she said.

They took the fast way, straight up. Then, Diane, Ivan, and Darko circled the Mont's summit, without talking, pretending to take in the view of Beaver Lake and downtown Montreal. They watched couples and families taking pictures of the views and each other, then slowly walking past the winged statue and into the chalet to get their bags of chips, sodas, or hot chocolate. None of them had said a word on the hike up the Mont. It had turned cold overnight.

"An American designed this," Darko said, reading Diane's guidebook. "Olmstead. The same guy who did Central Park."

Ivan was pacing. Diane stood near the ledge, staring out at the tops of trees and buildings.

"The lush forest was badly damaged by the Ice Storm of 1998," Darko read. "It has since largely recovered."

"You think you are only one to lie and cheat?" Ivan said at last to Diane. "You think you are only free one here?" Since that morning, his English began to break up. Darko stood beside Diane. He held her arm.

"Please," she said. "Stop."

"Did you know?" Ivan said, pacing in front of them. "Did you know that Cassandra is my other mistress? My Canadian woman?"

"That clothes designer? The redhead?" She tried to recall Cassandra, the woman who said *Katrina Patina*. She remembered the shoulders and the green dress. She couldn't tell if Ivan was telling the truth.

Darko said quietly, "My father. He's not a nice man."

Diane wondered if Darko had just come out and told his father that morning, or if Ivan simply knew when he saw Darko. Or maybe Ivan knew when he saw her.

She faced Ivan. "I don't know what else to say, Ivan. I thought we had agreed not to grow attached."

"You sicken me. You and your hurricane and your petty problems. A little trouble and you cry, *Wa wa wa, where is Mommy?* You have not seen war or bloodshed. You have not watched family members butchered."

"I can't stand when he does this," Darko said.

Standing next to Darko, Diane felt as though she were coming home late from a date, getting yelled at by a parent.

"I survived ten years of the Yugoslav Wars and no one even remembers them," Ivan said. "You Americans, so wrapped up in your 9/11 and your Katrina."

"Ivan, please."

"If it doesn't happen to American, it doesn't count to American." Ivan stopped, stepping aside to allow a hiker to snap a picture and pass.

Diane and Darko were standing so close to the edge. Ivan came close and jabbed his finger into Darko's chest, whispering something in Czech. Darko lowered his head, then stepped away, milling around the winged statue.

Ivan's lips touched Diane's cheek and ear. His breath was hot.

"My *son?*" He spit at her feet. "You two deserve each other."

He talked fast and in Czech. She stood leaning back, trying hard to keep her footing. If she fell to her death then and there, she realized how ridiculous her life would have been, how embarrassing, how there would be nothing to say or show for it.

"What is your awful American expression?" he said, his face red and sweaty. "*Grow up.* Grow up, Diane Zimmer."

He looked at her, and then stepped back. He took his jacket off and draped it over his shoulders like a cape." You find your own way back down. You don't have to do anything. You can do as you like. I have important work."

Nauseated, she watched him leave, his broad shoulders moving as his legs moved. He was so sure of his direction, and only moments ago seemed to have lost control. He was leaving her, more handsome than ever.

Darko came to her like some shy schoolboy. He held out her guidebook, which she took. He kissed her once, then twice on the cheek, and he walked away, going the opposite direction of his father's path.

What had she done? How could she right this? For an instant she recalled pulling off embroidered pillows, hand-stitched linens, and books caught, twisted, or impaled on a neighbor's wrought iron picket fence after the hurricane, as if unstabbing and untangling them would make a bit of difference in all that damage. Some messes can't be undone. How would she clean up her own life after this, at her age?

She looked around at other hikers and the view. How would she ever get off this mountain? The hike up had been no trouble. Getting down and finding her way back would be the hard part. She thought it better not to follow either Ivan or Darko. She went another way altogether, thinking all the paths surely led down. One path led to another and then to another until at last she grew clammy and exasperated.

This was not it. This was not it at all. She had gotten it all wrong. This path let out toward the schools. And that path led up again toward the hill with no view. Where was the path with the view? Where was the one that led her back to where she started? Where was the one with the giant cross, the one placed there to fulfill a vow when the founder of Montreal prayed to the Virgin Mary to stop a disastrous flood?

Fewer and fewer hikers passed, and she regretted that she had not asked for directions. It was getting cold and late and she was hungry. She slid on mud and wet leaves, then slipped and fell, rolling down a hill toward a small cliff, stopping herself just in time to look around and reconsider her situation. Below her was a kind of canyon on what felt like the edge of everything.

She saw her life as in a movie reel: she saw herself consuming newspapers, face creams, pasta, sweets, TV, pantyhose, and men, and she saw herself seated in the background in cafes, far away and removed from the main scenes, the main events. She had missed more than the hurricane—she had missed her marriage, her son, and time with her mother. She felt both betrayed and guilty of betrayal, but she wasn't sure at all how to right anything. Her cell phone rang inside her backpack and she answered it, laughing, feeling at once both lost and found. She heard the violin music on the line, the quirky, jerky jig. "Teddy? Mom? Oh, Mom."

"Are you crying?"

"No," she said, crying. It sickened Diane to think of her mother and son practicing their notes on the violin, hardening their tender fingertips for a ditty to play for her while she had been doing what she had been doing.

"I think I know what you're going through," her mother said.

Diane wanted to yell out *No, you don't. You have no idea what I'm going through or what kind of wreck I am*, but she stopped herself and said, "Oh, Mom. It's so great that you and Teddy are learning together."

"He's a wonderful boy," her mother said. "He reminds me of you, Diane. We're having such a nice time. But come home. We miss you." She heard static, and then, "I love you."

"Mom? Teddy? Can you hear me?" She heard her mother say something like *swallowtail*, and then the connection went bad and they were cut off entirely.

The air smelled of wet leaves and damp cement. She listened to a bird say over and over what sounded like *virtue virtue virtue.*

Years later, Diane would say everything had changed for her. She had not been in Chicago that night, the night her mother died of heart failure, but at the same time she had been very much with her. There on the edge, no bell went off, no light bulb, but Diane's memory of those moments on the Mont remained with her, though some of the details would change, and, through the years, she would recall some images more than others. She would point to this moment later, after the funeral, and during the drive back down south, and she would say that everything had changed for her then, right after she spoke to her mother.

Her shins were scraped and bleeding. She dabbed at the cuts with a gold, almost transparent leaf. Her son had learned to roller skate by falling and scraping his knees, only to get back up and start all over. She herself had taught him to swim, what she thought now might be her only gift to him. She taught him early because she knew he would be around water all his life. She wanted water to make her son as happy as it had made her. In the water, she had only to hold his head, telling him to lean back, his body would know what to do, and when it did, his legs and torso magically floating to the surface, she heard him laugh, saying *Ha!*

She stood up then and brushed away the dirt and debris from her jeans. She put her cell phone back into her bag, and wiped her nose with the back of her hand. Smoothing her hair into a ponytail, she stood and surveyed what was before her, looking for the way. Then she set forth and began her descent on yet another hidden footpath, thinking of her mother and her son, winding her way down the Mont, through the forest.

WHAT I WANT TO KNOW IS WHEN DID BARBARA MCINTOSH GET TO BE SO JEALOUS?

We're out there standing in front of what used to be St. Paul's where her little Cee Cee is swinging on monkey bars FEMA and The Home Depot put up, while I'm looking at the brown creases in Barbara's cleavage, swearing off ever sitting in the sun again. She starts in: *I got that invitation to some party celebrating your upcoming nuptials a few years back, but I guess you found out something about him, because there never was a marriage, was there?* She yells out for Cee Cee to be more careful, not to kick the little boy's eye out. Then she turns to me and says, *You just never know about a man, do you?*

I say something about not liking him anymore. I don't say anything about his drug habit or the dealing. Those don't even seem important now. I tell her I left and went to Indiana then I came back. I say it was like a holiday. We did go to the water park a lot.

She tells me her mother has Parkinson's. Since the storm, she says, and she's the *primary caregiver* now, not her sister. That's what she says. She rolls around in that word *primary*. They lost both houses in the hurricane, but they're rebuilding on her mother's property, old property high up and elevated above sea level, even though we both know that being in the cut glass set didn't make a bit of difference in the end. I don't say we used to call the people living on Barbara's side of town cake eaters, or that her mamma's old house needed a paint job way before the storm, or how I knew the columns in front were hollow and not made of wood at all. She doesn't say what I know she's thinking—that bitch Katrina was good for one thing, washing away all the riffraff, like me.

A little dog licks her leg probably because Barbara smells of the pink grapefruit soap the town is manufacturing now. Or is that the scent called *Energy* or *Gulf Waters*, the one that colored newscaster covering the aftermath went nuts over on that morning show? When Barbara talks baby talk to the dog, the dog can hardly stand it and pees.

She says her husband always thought people were so uppity here, but it's different now, after the hurricane. She says, *Aren't you near Menge in that first house on Second?*

Red brick ranch, I say.

Doesn't the train bother you?

We think it's soothing. Where do I get *soothing?*

Barbara looks to have put on twenty-five pounds of what everyone here calls the FEMA-fifteen, but even fat looks good on Barbara McIntosh—what with her streaked hair, frosted pink lipstick and the blue, flowered dress and black slip-ons. Me, I have so many hours as a black jack dealer at The Grand, there's hardly time to eat.

She calls out to her Cee Cee again, sweet this time, telling her to play nice with the little boy. He comes running. Barbara watches me wipe Billy's nose with the hem of my cut-offs. *Well he's a cutey isn't he? Aren't you a cutey?* she says, picking up her dog. Billy turns his father's black eyes on Barbara, then says *Come on Mamma, let's go,* and I love him more than ever for saying this. I tell him I'll buy him a snow cone. Later we'll go check out a movie from the double-wide that serves as the library where they keep the air at 63 degrees all summer.

Barbara says we ought to get our kids together and play. She puts her dog down. *You all should stop by the house.*

I tie Billy's shoes.

Barbara smiles, shakes her head, yanks on the little dog's chain, and says, *Seems like all our lives, the two of us have been trying to bust out of this place. We had our chance, you know, after the storm. Can you believe we both landed back here? Even you. You of all people.*

INSURANCE

Paul had never before lived so much indoors, nor had he spent so much time in rooms. He lay in bed and listened for his wife Mary's voice. He reached over and felt the blank space on the other side of the bed. He got up and tried to raise a window, but none of the windows in Diane's condo would open. As each day passed, the only thing Paul had to look forward to was the Scotch because then he might see Mary again.

In the kitchen of Diane's condo in Chicago, he poured himself a fourth drink, listening to Diane playing several messages on her answering machine from a man named Fred with three different phone numbers, asking to speak with Mary, wanting to know where he should send the report. It was confusing and painful to listen to someone saying his wife's name, and Diane stopped playing the machine.

It was spring, and even though they had buried her that winter, Paul sat at the kitchen table, and after he drank enough Scotch, there she sat, his wife Mary, young again and great with child, balancing the checkbook, paying bills, making it all work out, rearranging a scarf to cover a stain so that she could wear her good dress one extra time before taking it to the cleaners. She knew of such tricks, happy to joke about them with others only if she felt it was right to do so.

He was mourning everything. Of course he missed his wife. Of course her death made him immobile, but there was everything else too. There was the life he had with Mary, the young years and the middling years, and all those summers, when Mary wore pink clothes and gold jewelry and they were always tanned and smelling of suntan lotion so that by happy hour they really were celebrating each and every day's end and it felt as though they were going to be fifty-five forever. He wanted to go back to the Gulf Coast of Mississippi, but how could he without Mary? How could he do any of it without her?

"Knock Knock," his grandson Teddy said, sitting down now across from Paul, in the chair where Mary had just been. The boy had his math book with him and opened it there at the table.

"Who's there?" Paul said, sipping his Scotch.

"Interrupting cow."

"Interrupting cow . . ."

"Mooooo," Teddy said, not laughing, looking at Paul for a response.

"That was a bad one," Paul said.

"They're supposed to be bad."

The boy had taken to telling bad jokes to cheer Paul up. Paul looked at the figures and formulas penciled on Teddy's homework pages. Sometimes Paul couldn't help but wonder if the boy was a tad touched.

Teddy got up and answered the phone when it rang, then covered for Paul, saying he was "unavailable."

"Insurance man," Teddy said, as he hung up.

"Good. Time someone put *him* on hold." All those months of listening to menus, recordings, then getting re-routed or disconnected, Paul had nothing left to say to his insurance man whom he had grown to loathe more than was right. When he did finally get on the phone, the man could not complete a sentence, and his garbled fragments pained Paul. *I think it was all wind damage, and so forth maybe, you know. And so that's how your neighbor there supposedly got the insurance money, via the situation with the hurricane's wind damage as such.* The insurance man ended most thoughts with *all that and so on.*

Twenty years ago, Paul and Mary fell in love with the house in Pass Christian while they were on a business golf outing in Diamondhead. When Paul decided to retire, Mary renovated the place, and they sold their place in Texas to move to the coast full time. After the hurricane, Paul didn't have enough money to cover both their living expenses and the cost of rebuilding everything. He was well past the point when he was making less than $100 a week, but he was not past fearing those days.

The insurance company paid only a fraction of what the house was worth, so he had not been able to rebuild the house for his wife before she died, nor had he even been able to promise her that he would in fact rebuild because he wasn't sure if they could afford it any more. He was all out of promises. He hadn't even been able to bury his wife in the town she loved most. *All that and so on.*

The first time he held the gun to his head, Paul sat in the chair in Diane's guest room, wondering for a split second why he was thinking of shooting himself, and why, say, George Bush, Dick Cheney, or that Donald Rumsfeld weren't. Why was it that the people who shot themselves were hardly ever the people who should shoot themselves? Why hadn't O. J. shot himself? Wasn't shooting one's self sometimes exactly the thing to do?

He held the barrel to his nose, his mouth, and finally to his temple, leaning into the cold metal warming to his skin. It was a service pistol, an Enfield with a wood handle from the 1930s his father gave him, but for what, he could not recall.

Everything had come to an end so fast and in such a big way. They made a promise. When the big one came, they'd stay, and if the house went down, they would go down with it. That was the promise. But on August 28, after they boarded up, Mary walked through their darkened home, and she said she wanted to leave. That's all she had to say. So they left. They waited in the lines for the gas, they endured the interstate traffic, and after they heard what had happened, that their town was gone, they just kept driving, barely talking, slowly making their way up to Diane's place in Chicago. Still later, everything spiraled out of control. Diane left the country with a new boyfriend, Paul and Mary were left parenting their grandson, Teddy, and then Mary died. She died. She left without him.

In his mind, Paul knew everything came to an end eventually—childhood, relationships with parents, lives. Before, Paul looked from a distance upon the ends of friends' lives, careers, companies, even his own daughter's marriage. He concluded that ending wasn't something anybody wanted. Even at the end of phone calls or a restaurant meal, some moron would say, "Have a nice day." What ever happened to a simple *Good-bye*? Even though people said they wanted *closure*—Jesus, how he hated that word—nobody wanted anything to be over.

It was nearly five p.m. and though he had that all-gone feeling, and he held the gun, he became preoccupied with a throbbing tooth and he put down his gun.

He had lost a tooth and his straight nose to football way back in high school, and his father wouldn't pay for a new bridge or any of the dental work, so his mouth always bothered him. Paul felt his teeth with interest. How did this happen that one day you were healthy and married, and the next day you woke up old, alone, sour-smelling, your tooth aching as though your life had been a dream? He bothered the tooth with his tongue, causing a pain, which worked as well as smelling salts.

Paul poured a Scotch and waited for Mary who did not come and sit with him. He replayed Diane's answering machine and listened to Fred's steady voice. Then he picked up the phone and returned the phone call meant for Mary.

After Paul spelled it all out, venting that his home got hit by the hurricane, and his wife died, and with her, their marriage of fifty-five years, he listened to Fred's apologies.

"I'm a forensic engineer," Fred said. "Your wife hired me. I do hurricane damage investigations."

"She never told me about you," Paul said. "I was taking care of this."

"She didn't want to upset you because she knew the insurance company was dicking you around."

Paul couldn't help but laugh in disgust. "I'm hanging up."

"Look, your wife asked me to go down, investigate the remains of your house. Are you still there? Here's the bottom line: the wind lifted that new boardwalk the city built in front of your house. The timbers from the boardwalk breached the house, and *then* the water came. You follow? Wind damage first, water second. If you give me your insurance company's name, I'll send the report. It's a thick report. And your wife already paid for it."

The refrigerator hummed. Someone was playing a violin in another apartment unit. Paul looked out over Lake Michigan, wishing it was the Gulf. He didn't know what to say. He gave Fred the name and address of his insurance company and the name of the man who spoke in fragments. Paul had already lost his home, most of his equity, and his wife, what else did he have to lose?

"That bridge?" Fred said. "Your wife asked about it. The one to Bay St. Louis? They rebuilt it. It's open now."

That night, as the three of them gathered for dinner, a light snow fell even though it was March. Paul ate meat again. He told Diane and Teddy how he had in mind to return to Neshoba County, Mississippi, the cradle of his ancestors. They could all go, fly to Memphis, then rent a car, and head down Highway 55 during Teddy's spring break. Paul had always flown, but now he thought to drive through his own state.

"*How Time is slipping underneath our Feet: Unborn Tomorrow and dead Yesterday, Why fret about them if Today be sweet!*" Paul said.

"What's that from?" Teddy asked.

"When I was in college I memorized parts of *The Rubáiyát*, a long poem by a Persian fellow named Omar Khayyám, to get dates with all the pretty girls," Paul said. "It worked better then all that 'seize the day' stuff."

Teddy tilted his head, and Diane messed his hair. "You don't need to worry about girls and dating quite yet."

"Soon," Paul said, sounding ghost-like, making Teddy laugh. "Soon dear boy."

"Wasn't Omar Khayyám a mathematician?" Teddy asked.

"The very same one," Paul said. "You wouldn't be suffering algebra or geometry or cubrics or whatever you're suffering if it weren't for old Omar."

"I *like* math."

"Could we not talk about math or science for a while?"

Diane had just broken up with the geek physics professor who wore turtlenecks, and she seemed more than ready to leave town. In fact, she looked younger and relieved as they began to talk about the trip.

"*Better be merry with the fruitful grape than sadden after none, or bitter, Fruit.*"

"All right all right, we're going!" Diane said.

"Omar liked wine," Paul whispered to Teddy. "A lot."

Diane packed and made preparations with the usual fuss. She even left an elaborate outgoing message on her voicemail, telling who ever called how she could be reached by email or cell phone.

"Why not tell them to use a bullhorn?" Paul said, listening to her two weeks later on the morning of their departure. He couldn't wait to get out of all the buzzing, jingling and ringing of downtown Chicago. He had showered and put on a button-down shirt, slow because he was out of the habit of dressing. He was reasonably good-looking with his blue eyes and white hair. He had managed to keep his weight down and he knew how to carry himself and how to look like he didn't care what anybody thought. This was what Mary told him once, and he felt better about everything when she had said this. She could do that, Mary could. Turn everything around for him so that he felt he could do anything.

§

"The trees are so straight here," Teddy said, later from the backseat, trying too hard to make conversation as they drove farther south past the Memphis airport. "They just go up and down."

"They'll do that," Paul said.

Diane sat already asleep in the front passenger seat, her GPS and a map open on her lap.

"Knock knock," Teddy said.

"Who's there?" Paul said.

"Buddha."

"Buddha who?"

"Buddha this slice of bread for me."

As soon as they crossed the border, then headed east, toward Neshoba County, they stopped at Spanky's for gas and coffee. Inside, "Sugar Shack" was playing, a song Paul hadn't heard since he and Mary danced to it at a party in Jackson during those crew-cut years in the early sixties.

They drove on. They passed boys Teddy's age hot-dogging on four-wheelers. They passed children jumping on trampolines out in front of their homes. They passed farmers plowing open fields and they passed ditched cars covered with kudzu.

"Why do you wave?" Teddy asked when Paul waved to passing cars and drivers waved back.

"It's what we do down here. We're kindlier in the South."

Diane said something sarcastic under her breath, her eyes still shut.

Outside Philadelphia, Mississippi, not very far from where the three Civil Rights boys were murdered, they stood in the Mount Zion church cemetery before Paul's great-grandfather's grave. Paul told Teddy that Coy Zimmer fought in the Revolutionary War as an officer under General George Washington, then settled here in Neshoba County where he could lead a peaceful life with his two families, one with his wife, Eva, the other with his mistress, a Negress named Red Apple.

"You had to tell him that?" Diane said.

"He's old enough."

"Was Coy a racist?" Teddy asked.

Paul thought about this. Paul's father liked to insist that it was fashionable back then to have a black mistress. He hadn't said anything about the children though. "I guess it depends on how you look at it."

Teddy read the tombstone out loud. *I have fought a good fight, I have finished my course, I have kept the faith.*

Next to Coy's grave lay his wife's, Eva.

Paul's father used to take Paul here regularly when he was growing up. The last time Paul was here, he had taken his father. Paul had just turned fifty-five and he had made his fourth million.

"Looks like you're gettin' beyond your raisin'," his father had said, hawking and spitting graveside. Paul supposed some could have taken this as a compliment, but Paul knew better. To Mississippians like his father, bettering one's self was not always something one ought to strive for.

Teddy moved to where Paul's father was buried and Paul said all the respectful things one should say about one's dead father.

Twice his father visited Paul and Mary after they had moved in permanently on the coast. The first visit, he kicked a door, claiming it didn't work. When Mary made crabmeat omelets for breakfast one morning, Paul's father said he'd had better in New Orleans. On the second visit, his father opened the French doors to piss off the front porch and into the front lawn, triggering the alarm system in the middle of the night. Later, after his father left, Paul saw Mary on her hands and knees in the guest bathroom cleaning up his father's urine. Mary didn't say anything, but to Paul, it looked as though a dog had used the room, pissing on the floors and even on the walls. His father had either lost his mind or was trying to tell him something, something as basic as, *Piss on you and all that you've worked for.*

In his later years, his father befriended Preacher Killen, one of the men charged and finally sentenced years later with killing those three Civil Rights boys. When Paul had come upon Killen and his father together in his father's den, huddled on the sofa like two lovers, he was struck by how much they looked alike. His father had not been a racist when Paul's mother was alive. She had been the civilizing influence with her cut glass and coconut cakes, sifted fine. When she died, Paul began to overhear his father refer to King as Martin Luther Coon. Then finally, when his father died at age 90, Paul was ashamed to find not so much sorrow, but relief over his death.

Was this Paul's fate now that Mary was gone? Was Paul going to become his father like so many other men were destined to become?

"It's so nice out here," Diane said, looking out over the cemetery.

They got back in the car and Paul keyed the ignition.

"Knock knock."

"Not again, Teddy. Please," Diane said. Some weather was coming.

"Who's there," Paul said.

"Boo."

"Boo who?"

"Sorry I made you cry."

Paul had in mind to go into the town of Philadelphia and see if an eatery he liked was still open. He told Teddy about growing up in Neshoba County, how other children thought his name Zimmer sounded German, or worse, Jewish, and they marched around him, stiff-legged and lock-kneed, saying *hut hut hut*. He was born in 1932, sixty-seven years after the Civil War. He knew about the P word, *prejudice*, and he knew about the N word. He had a good argument for and against both. He'd seen a KKK rally at the courthouse in his teens. He and his pal, Ed, called them *bed sheeters*. Later Ed became a Grand Kleagle or some other nonsense. Paul didn't tell his grandson this.

Paul was a young man living in Jackson when the Civil Rights boys were found. It was craziness then, craziness that no one wanted to talk about anymore. After Bobby Kennedy got shot, Paul recalled sitting down at a Kiwanas' rubber-chicken lunch, and the guy next to him, a client, asked for some sweet iced tea, then said, "Two down, one to go."

That very night, right after Mary said she wasn't going to read the Jackson papers anymore, she said as an afterthought, *why not leave?*

"They're blaming everything on 'The Negro Problem,'" she said, and didn't that have a Nazi ring to it? And wasn't that going to lead to something like "The Final Solution?" In later years, Paul saw how easy it was for their southern friends to get behind this war against terrorism. All foreigners were essentially terrorists to Mississippians. Funny how they could never see themselves as terrorists. Not even during the 60s when that was exactly what so many of them had become. The young now saw the 1960s as simply unpleasant. The real ugliness was lost on them, which was just as well. It had been insane, indescribable and remarkably dangerous for everyone. Ross Barnett and Allan Thompson. The governor and the mayor. The leadership and everyone in between, they were all buffoons. Doing business there was embarrassing. After the KKK bombed the temple down the street, he and Mary decided to leave Mississippi. It was the principle of the thing—first the people of Mississippi went after the civil rights kids, outsiders mostly, then they started going after their own, people who had businesses and who had lived in Mississippi for years and years. He'd had enough of the lunacy. He wasn't that kind of southern. It occurred to him then, in 1967, and now, in this, the 21st century: they eat their own here. Who knew what else they were capable of?

He found a sales position with a financial firm in Lubbock, Texas, then the oil business lured him away. Mary cheerfully engaged with every woman's group in town and they barely took notice of the dust and all that hard red clay. Her optimism propelled him to dig in at work and those years were boon years.

The rain started fast as spring rains did down here. The sky burst open and poured forth water in sheets. Paul slowed and so too did the rain. There was a steady, light drizzle and the sun peaked out, though it continued to rain.

If Mary was still alive and with him, they might be driving now, full from crabmeat or steak. They would be at the coast and the sun would be setting, turning the water silver and red and Paul would inevitably recall the lines from *The Rubáiyát of Omar Khayyám* and say, "*Ah, Moon of my Delight who know'st no wane.*" And Mary, she would touch the pearls he'd given her and laugh and nudge him, drawing closer to his knee, and his heart would fill up with such happiness. Did she know? She must have known. Their daughter married, their grandson born, they were alone and together again, and they were perfect. Perfect.

When Paul saw the black, wiry thing, not quite dog nor wolf, come slinking out of the woods like that, he didn't know what the hell it was at first, slouching toward some road kill.

"Just a fife," he said, but Diane and Teddy both said *don't hit it!* And he swerved to miss it, and in the swerving, the car screeched and skidded, then spun around and went off the road and straight into a muddy ditch.

They were still upright and Paul tried to back out, but the wheels spun in the muck.

"I knew something like this would happen," Dianne said.

"Are we OK?" Paul said, wondering if he was, in fact, OK.

They got out and checked themselves. It felt strange and good to be out of the car and standing, even in the mud. Paul could smell the wet soil. A man came out of a pawn shop not but a few feet away, and Paul could hear the man's voice. "Ya'll need help?"

Guns and stuffed deer heads lined the walls of Beem's Pawn, Gun & Discount, and the TV was on a program about bass fishing. Right away Paul saw that the fellow who ran the place was a good old boy and Paul brought up growing up in these parts before he said anything about not hitting the dog.

The man tried to talk Paul into going to the hospital, but even though he felt stiff, Paul insisted he'd had enough of doctors. Diane and Teddy nodded in agreement.

"I should have just run it over," Paul said of the fife, making the others around the counter laugh. There were three men there, Indians all of them and they were already heading out the door to push the car out of the ditch. Paul supposed he was to go with the men, but he didn't want to, and he stayed behind with the owner, leaning on the counter.

"Grandfather," Teddy said, sounding especially Northern and nassally now. "It was a *dog*."

"A mongrel," Paul said, making the owner laugh further. "All the more reason."

Teddy stood, looking confused or disappointed, Paul could not say which. A young Choctaw girl, about Teddy's height, stood nearby, testing out a pair of stickball sticks. Diane began to wander about the store in the way she had of being both spacey and attentive to merchandise.

"Oh look," she said from within the aisles. "Choctaw baskets."

Paul leaned on the counter splattered with hunting pictures, and he listened as the owner of the pawn shop told him about what he shot, where, when, and how. Paul was happy here. He considered a future without Mary in his south, growing old, taking strolls across civil war battle sites, or better yet, looking out over the Mississippi Sound toward Ship Island, to Fort Massachusetts, even knowing that once upon a time young prisoners suffered in the heat, drinking water poisoned with lead.

Then Paul remembered: his father had grown old and bitter with hatred after *his* wife died, would Paul?

The owner told Paul that they had a woman in the back making those baskets his daughter liked so well. She was eighty-two and probably one of the last to know how to make them. The Indian girl asked Teddy if he wanted to see her baby squirrel. Teddy looked at his grandfather and Paul nodded and said he'd come with. He wanted an excuse not to check on the men pushing the car out of the ditch.

The girl led them to a separate structure in the back of the store, one with a corrugated tin roof. A dog followed them out, licking at Teddy's legs, but the girl shooed him away, calling the dog by an Indian name.

They greeted an old woman there in the middle of a warm, damp room making baskets. The old woman smiled a toothless smile, and then went back to her half-woven basket, one with a complicated chessboard design.

Paul thought of the Choctaw women he used to see walking down the road, baskets on their head, babies at their back, their men riding horses. They were quiet people, and most merchants knew better than to speak with them. They liked to come in, gather their items, then pay in cash, without a word spoken. Paul recalled then that a Choctaw man found the burned-out car belonging to the three Civil Rights workers, after they went missing. Paul imagined that when the FBI went to the swamp, those Indians didn't speak, but just pointed to the spot where the car sat sinking in the muddy sludge.

On top of a heating pad in a shoebox under a cut-up moccasin lay a hairless two-day old squirrel, its eyes shut tight. The black-eyed girl picked up the rat-like thing as though it were her own baby, and stuck a tiny bottle of formula in its mouth.

"We found him in the yard after yesterday's storm. He's getting hair, see? He's coming along. The ants were getting him here," she said, pointing to the raw spot under its arm where skin had been eaten pink.

"Wow," Teddy said, leaning closer to get a better look.

"I know," the girl said. "Isn't it cool?"

Paul hadn't told Mary about the other phone calls. He wanted to spare her the details of the storm and the aftermath and about their good friends down the street, the McKinneys, who had stayed. For eight hours, they sat on the steps going up to their attic as the water rose in their home, and when Ella saw their wedding pictures floating, she stepped into the water to gather them. Even though they survived the storm, Ella died two weeks later, her legs eaten up by the flesh-eating bacteria she'd gotten from stepping into the water.

There were other friends he had called too, friends who had quietly died or moved away, most ending up in assisted care retirement homes, resigned to having cocktails at 4:40 instead of 5, dinner at 6, bed by 9. Over the phone, Paul could tell they only shook their heads now about the botched war and government, and the Arabs buying up their coast. Their anger had vanished and they didn't care about anything, as long as they got their free popcorn at happy hour while they watched their plasma TVs, or joined their wives for shopping or bridge. They seemed so much better equipped to move on with this last phase of their lives.

Teddy couldn't keep his eyes off the pathetic quivering squirrel and neither could Paul.

"We looked up how to care for him online," the girl said, dampening a Q-tip with a drop of water, then rubbing the cotton end on the squirrel's privates until the thing peed and shat. "It's like what cats do for their kittens. You have to make him go to the bathroom." Watching the girl do this disturbed Paul. His loins ached, making him ashamed and nauseated.

"Gross," Teddy said, watching closely as the half-dead squirrel did its business.

Paul sat down, near the old woman who was making a basket so tightly woven you could drink from it. The red and black arrow shapes were all going the same direction, all in a row, their pattern repeated in each continuous row, over and over, even on the bottom.

Paul took off his shoes. He needed to feel the cool floor on the soles of his feet. The old woman moved her long, gray braid off her shoulder.

Mary had always kept her hair up in a bun, and then at night when she unpinned it, she brushed it all out past her shoulders. For years it was blond, then it was white. He couldn't recall the in-between years, the years when the colors mixed, for surely there had been such years in between. Had he not noticed? Had he paid enough attention to her hair, her shoulders, her eyes, her lips?

She never much cared for jewelry, so birthdays and Christmas were troublesome and he never knew what to give her. He gave her paintings, books, and eventually a pearl necklace, which she took to wearing to the Yacht Club on Friday or Saturday nights. All of these gifts were in the Gulf or out there somewhere north in DeLisle.

He married Mary because he didn't want to live without her. She pleased him so much, he wanted to please her back and it seemed to work this way all through the years.

When she touched him, even in the later, older years, the place where she had her hand would turn warm, always, even if they were arguing. His body knew her. His body remembered her. His body—blood, bones, muscle, skin, groin, all of it, everywhere on him—missed her.

"You OK, grandfather?" Teddy touched Paul's arm.

For a moment, Paul thought he had passed out, but he had not. His tongue felt for his tooth, and for the pain that worked as smelling salts.

"Mom's looking for you," Teddy said.

Diane stood at the door in the dim light. She had inherited her mother's fine straight nose and solid cheekbones. She was tall and slim. Handsome was the word, but not lovely. His daughter didn't have the sweetness that so many men enjoy. She wasn't soothing or maternal, but she was never an embarrassment to look upon. Sometimes he looked at Diane and wondered who this young woman was. With her, Paul felt it was too late. Maybe not so much with the boy.

"It's for you," she said, handing Paul her cell phone.

He stood up to take the call, listening to the voice on the phone telling him in incomplete sentences that he was sorry about his wife.

Paul recognized the voice of his insurance man, the man who spoke in fragments. He told Paul he had gotten the thick report, and that after much discussion, they had a new offer. He gave Paul a figure, a sum half of what the house was worth, but more than the previous offer. Paul looked at the woman and her basket, the girl, and the homeless, motherless squirrel, who had been blown out of his nest.

"It's a start," Paul said.

His insurance man said something about how this was still a very *liquid* situation and Paul knew he meant *fluid*. Either way, it was a poor choice of words, given the situation, but the man's way of speaking didn't grate on Paul's nerves as much as it had before.

When he had ended the call, Paul turned to his grandson, standing before him. At some point, the boy had combed his hair straight back so that his ears stuck out. He had a soft, pudding face Paul chalked up to being around too many women. He was becoming a handsome boy, still awkward now because he did not yet know how to carry himself. He should have a sport. That would improve his bearing.

Paul knew then that they would drive down farther to the coast. Once there, they would all view the damage for the last time before they got started with the rebuilding. He was no geezer. He was seventy-five years old, and by God, he was going to live out what was left of him in that house on the coast.

It had stopped raining. The Choctaw men had gotten their car out of the ditch. All was well, they said. Paul bought his daughter $700 worth of Choctaw baskets because he felt guilty for the accident. Diane actually smiled, saying she remembered how much her mother had loved these kinds of baskets. Paul knew she didn't need or maybe even want the baskets. It was a private matter between mother and daughter Paul could and could not make sense of.

As he paid, the man behind the counter suggested they stay the night at the Golden Moon, which he considered the better of the two Choctaw casinos in the Pearl River Resort.

Paul gave Diane the car keys. "Your turn," he said, and she looked at him.

"What's that saying about having to get back in the saddle?" she said.

"That works for horseback riding, not for driving cars or getting married again."

She raised an eyebrow and gave them each a stack of baskets to carry to the car.

They drove west toward Carthage, all of them spotting the hotel jutting out of Highway 16 like some Oz. Paul supposed the Blue Moon had a Choctaw meaning and he meant to ask at the front desk or look it up some day, some time.

Inside, it was lit up, noisy, and crowded just like at The Grand, but the games were called things like Xenon. Choctaw names were everywhere as a kind of payback—the casinos, the banks and stores, there was even the Dancing Rabbit Golf Course.

A voice on the sound system said *so many temptations to indulge, it's hard to settle on just one thing. Choices are available . . .*

Diane checked them in and they walked a good deal past the gaming and the gamblers toward the elevators.

So many people and so much noise. It was dizzying.

There they all were, together at last at the Golden Moon—Christians, Jews, Choctaws, blacks, whites, washed, unwashed, sinners and saved, rich, poor, skinny and fat, all here amidst the Hot Dollars and Moon Shadow Slots looking for Rapid Redemptions and something to eat.

A TV set over the bar was running a stickball game between *Oka Homma* and *Bok Chitto*. Some of the Choctaw players were barefooted, some wore Nikes.

At the elevators, a white man asked a black man if he was having any luck.

The black man shrugged and said *A little bit on the roulette*.

They stood in front of the elevators, listening to the squeaks and moans of the machinery echoing in the shafts.

Diane whispered something about so many large people.

The elevators moaned louder. Paul thought he heard Teddy say, "Grandmother?"

Paul looked around. He and Mary had seen the very worst of this state and the very best.

"Knock-knock," Paul said.

The boy looked unsure. "Who's there?"

"Ivan," Paul said.

The elevator doors opened.

"Ivan who?"

Diane's left eyebrow lifted.

The people stepped out of the elevator and they stepped in, moving to the back, waiting for the doors to shut.

"Ivan to be alone," Paul said in a Transylvanian accent.

The boy looked surprised then said *Ha,* the smile still on his lips as the doors shut.

"Really?" Diane said. "Do you, Dad?"

Paul smiled at his daughter, then put his hand on Teddy's shoulder. "What chances you think that squirrel has?"

The elevators moaned and whistled and Paul thought of all the Choctaw there, wondering who of them could hear their ancestors in all this noise.

"Oh, it'll live," Teddy said, moving closer, looking up at the numbers as they began to rise.

AFTERMATH LOUNGE

Catch stepped out of his trailer and saw the girl alone on the beach across the highway. She was wading ankle deep in the Gulf, wearing a light brown bikini the color of her skin. Catch hadn't seen many people on the beach in a long time, not since the hurricane, the hurricane most people in town couldn't stand to call by name anymore.

The bulldozers were still going at it next door. Several of them had come to tear down what was left of a house, moving the debris out toward the split-open highway, beeping as they reversed, filling the morning air with the stink of diesel exhaust. You didn't complain though. You were supposed to be grateful. Blue tarps still diapered some roofs, and everywhere Catch turned were the white portable storage units called "pods." A black man he did not recognize was painting the big wrought iron gate next door, even though the gate's house was gone.

It was almost summer, more than eight months after the storm, and still the population of Pass Christian had not achieved the critical mass necessary for a grocery store. You could get cereal, milk, coffee, and bread at the Quick-Stop, but no eggs. It was hard to stay supplied, and Catch was out of everything—food, booze, weed.

He swatted something on the back of his neck. The flies had gotten fatter; the dragonflies bigger and the wasps, too. From the bottom of his bare foot, Catch peeled a torn page from a book. None of the sentences on the yellowed scrap were whole, but he played at trying to make sense of them. *A liaison with . . . greatly as well. He is a . . . man. His enthusiasms are . . . generous with his women . . . money from Anna . . . and the will to survive. He shrugged. She vibrated . . . Johnny.* He laughed to himself and put the paper in his pocket with all the other scraps he'd picked up the day before. There was paper everywhere, swollen and dry: mail, Bibles, maps, grocery lists, a library's worth of books.

Catch situated himself on a tree swing to put on his socks and boots. His trailer was in the Zimmers' yard, near what was left of their home. He had worked for the Zimmers as a yardman and as a handy man for the better part of fifteen years. They'd evacuated before the storm, but he stayed behind to take care of their house.

A small guesthouse—really a former slave quarters—behind the main house had saved him. It was on high ground, farther back from the beach. He'd waited out the storm in it like some trapped animal, standing on top of the toilet, watching the water rise, listening to the whole town come to pieces outside in the dark. He'd waited hours for the winds to die down. Only then had he stepped down into the swirling black water to unshutter the door and see that everywhere the ocean was receding from a world that had been blown apart. For days afterward his skin had been covered with a thin layer of salt.

Catch had lost his home and everything in it. The entire Gulf Coast—everything he knew, really—had been flattened. He'd remained on the Zimmers' property to keep looters out and deal with the utility crews and the inspectors and such. Mr. Zimmer had decided to rebuild on the same lot, not a hundred yards farther back from the beach. Catch thought he was nuts. He didn't know what he wanted to do himself. He had to consider his options. He planned to look up his ex-wife, Norma—if he could learn where she was. He had seen her once in passing the previous Christmas, but otherwise, they had not spoken in ten years. Last he'd heard, she was raising her friend's baby in an apartment in Gulfport.

Catch was hungry, but he hated to cook at the community grill, where people came with their plastic containers or Ziploc bags or slippery packages of raw meat. The men and women would stand shoulder to shoulder, sharing survival stories and lists of complaints while they pushed their meat around on the grill, careful not to touch anyone else's.

Remembering that the Sonic drive-through had re-opened in Long Beach, Catch got in his truck—a rental from a place in Hattiesburg—nodded to the black man still painting the fence, and pulled out onto the torn-up highway. Parked beside the road was an unfamiliar car that he figured belonged to the girl in the bikini. It had Louisiana license plates and a bumper sticker that said, *Jesus is coming. Look busy.* The back seat was loaded down with what looked to be all her personal effects. Catch had picked up that expression—"personal effects"—along with "critical mass" and others, since the hurricane: *The population has to reach a critical mass before rebuilding can begin.* And *Sir, you need to get all your personal effects out of here so we can begin the bulldozing.*

Beside the highway Catch saw all the signs saying, "We'll be Back!" On one house someone had spray-painted, "I will lie down to bleed awhile, and then get up and fight again." Then there were the signs offering services for mold removal, demolition, and Jesus—and some newer ones advertising palm trees for sale, for property owners ready to rebuild and relandscape.

At the Sonic, Catch ordered a toaster sandwich from a roller-skating waitress. Some old eighties song was playing, and he tried not to stare at the woman eating in the car parked next to his. Her face was swollen and bandaged, and she was having a tough time chewing. After his food came, he rolled up the windows and drove back while he ate.

As he approached the Zimmers' house, Catch saw the girl in the bikini coming up the beach with a plastic bag full of clothes in one hand and a dog, a black Rottweiler, following menacingly at her ankles. She looked like a zombie out of some old horror movie, walking slow and steady with her arms out in front of her. She should have kept on that way, but she panicked and ran, and then the dog leaped, and she was down, the dog straddling her chest, going for her face and neck.

Catch stopped his truck in the middle of the highway, got out, and ran to the girl. He kicked the sweet Jesus out of that dog. He kicked it hard in the ribs with the toe of his boot, and it let out a yelp and backed up but didn't go away. When Catch bent to help the girl up, the dog came charging.

Catch could see only its teeth and eyes and broad chest and black cinder-block head. There was a powerful smell of dog crap, piss, and dead animal. Catch kicked the dog again, harder this time, aiming for the chest, and with a whimper the dog fell back.

"Can you stand up?" Catch said to the girl, his eyes still on the dog. He heard her moan, and from the corner of his eye he saw her rise, then fall back down. Clutching the plastic bag to her chest, she whispered, "Help me," as if she didn't want the dog to hear.

He backed over to her and picked her up in his arms. The dog growled and bared its teeth as Catch walked away with the girl.

"Yeah, that's right," he said to the dog. "I'm leaving with supper."

A high moan emerged from the bloody, sand-covered girl in his arms.

When Catch got to his truck, he put her in and shut the door. The dog followed close, sniffing the ground where Catch had walked, licking the blood that had dripped from the girl. Catch turned his key in the ignition, and the dog trotted to the highway, lifted its hind leg, and pissed on the asphalt, as if to say, *This is my highway, my beach*. Any other time, Catch would have laughed, but now he wished he had a gun.

The girl's ankles were bleeding, and the dog had bitten her forehead. She shook and cried and whispered over and over, "Thank you. Thank you."

"I'm taking you to a FEMA tent in town," he said. "You're going to be OK."

Catch felt as though his bones were being ground to bits each time he drove by the rows of army tents on Second Street. The sight put him in what he called his "Vietnam mode." He pulled up next to a tent with a red cross on it and helped the girl inside. Right away a fat, pale medic came to them, snapped on his gloves, and started cleaning the girl up, dabbing at her wounds with antiseptic. None were so deep that she'd need stitches. She'd had a recent tetanus shot, she said, right after the storm, when they were giving them out for free. She said that the dog hadn't looked rabid, but who knew? They gave her the first shot anyway. She was small-boned and thin, but not frail, maybe thirty, with big eyes and freckles across her nose. Her lips were badly chapped. There was a tattoo of the sun on her right forearm, and her eyebrow was pierced.

"It's good y'all's trees are coming back," she said to the medic.

All around them the army green canvas walls flapped in the breeze. Catch eyed the needles and syringes and the bottles of pills in the medic's box.

A policeman came to ask the girl questions. She whispered her name: Nancy Cunningham. When he asked her address, she said, "My house is gone. I live in my car."

The medic wrapped her ankles while the cop, whose name was Martin Ladiné, talked into the walkie-talkie strapped to his shoulder. He and Catch knew each other from back when Catch had been married to Norma and she'd gotten into trouble with drugs and run off with her dealer. Catch asked Martin what the hell they planned to do about that dog, and Martin said animal-rights volunteers were quarantining stray dogs.

"That dog bit her ankles to get her down," Catch said. "Then he went at her head. That was an attack." The wind was picking up, making the tents flap louder. "That dog's hungry and mean, and it's gonna kill someone."

"Come on now, Catch," Martin said, putting a hand on his shoulder. "All this mess would drive any animal to madness—or maybe to bite at a pretty girls' legs." He winked.

Catch mumbled, "The hell."

The girl named Nancy Cunningham stood carefully, then sure and straight. The medic gave her a handful of "samples"—pills packed in neat rows of plastic and foil—and told her to take one whenever she felt any pain. As he said this, he looked at Catch. The medic reminded her the pills were for medical use only.

"Come on," Catch said to Nancy. "I bet you're hungry."

When they got into his truck, Nancy put on her clothes—the ones she'd been carrying in the plastic bag—over her bikini: worn bluejeans, flip-flops, and a yellow shirt that she tied into a knot at her midriff. Her brown bangs covered a good portion of the bandage across her forehead. She brought her feet up in the seat so that he saw her gauze-wrapped ankles and her dirty toes.

"You feel OK?" he asked.

"I'm OK."

"Hungry?"

"You don't have to feed me."

"There's a place up the road," he said, starting his engine. "They serve a good dinner."

Catch drove up Second Street and turned on North. Near Henderson Avenue they passed the boat in the tree and the boarded-up house spray-painted, "Nationwide 911 Help." He parked in a gravel lot beside a corrugated-tin building.

"What's this place?" Nancy asked.

He pointed to the sign on the door: *KAFE KATRINA AND THE AFTERMATH LOUNGE: WE'RE COOKING UP A STORM.*

"That's funny," she said, not laughing.

Catch opened the restaurant door for her, and people looked up when they entered. He'd forgotten what that was like, walking into a place with a woman. He ran his fingers through his hair. He wasn't half bad looking—old, but not too old. No gut yet. The diners were the same people Catch saw every day: the volunteers, the builders from Hattiesburg, the Yacht Club folks taking a break from the double-wide that now served as their club house.

Captain Smith, who wanted to be mayor, came over to tell Catch they were looking for people, vets especially, to help clean up the veterans' cemetery in time for Memorial Day. Before the storm Smith had never spoken to Catch. Now everyone raised their hands to each other, relieved, it seemed, to see a fellow survivor. Catch said he didn't care about the cemetery or Memorial Day. He was in no mood for remembering war. He had been through that and then some, and he told Smith as much.

Smith put his arm around Catch's shoulder and said, with a glance at Nancy, "That's OK, Catch. I see you got your hands full."

Catch sat down with Nancy, and she ordered the catfish with Creole tomato sauce. They drank cold beer and her food came fast. Catch liked watching Nancy eat. She alternated bites of everything on her plate—catfish, potatoes, greens— saving her square of cornbread for last. Then she ordered blackberry cobbler with vanilla ice cream for dessert. By God, she could eat. Catch didn't order anything. His teeth hurt. He would have to drive to Jackson to see a dentist, and the thought made him sour.

When Nancy had eaten everything on her plate, she leaned back and said, "Yeah, all that anger has to go somewhere," as though Catch had asked her a question. Maybe she had gotten like him, he thought: talking to herself.

"These volunteers, they're just tourists," she said, leaning in closer to him. "They come and want to eat seafood and drink all night, and I'm thinking, Now wait a minute. You can't come here and act like nothing happened. Fix it, paint it, move on. You know? Like, the world can't just keep going— not after this."

"I hear you."

Martin and the medic they had just seen came in and sat down.

"How come that cop didn't go out after that dog?" Nancy asked.

"He will at some point. I guess a dog's the least of his worries. He's seen a lot." Catch told her about how Martin and his men had holed up in the county library during the storm, and when the water had gotten too high, they'd had to shoot out the windows so they could swim away. They held on to the tops of trees until the storm subsided.

Nancy said she was hoping to find work at one of the casinos that were reopening on the coast. Catch said he guessed all the casinos would come back even bigger soon enough. She asked about his place, and he told her it was gone too. He shrugged and said it was just stuff anyhow. No loved ones. He thought of how *loved ones* was beginning to sound too much like *personal effects*. He told her about the old couple he worked for, the Zimmers, and how for a while he'd lived in a tent inside their ruined house. Now he had the FEMA trailer.

"So you're not unhappy here in Pass Christian?" she asked, pronouncing the name of the town like a Northerner would: *Chris*-chen. He taught her to pronounce it like a local: Chris-*chan*.

"It was named for Nicholas Christian Ladner, who settled at Cat Island in 1745," he said.

"You know a lot." He couldn't tell if this was a good or a bad thing.

Nancy had come from New Orleans, and he told her he'd spent time there when he was young, before he'd gone off to war.

"The Gulf War?" she said.

He laughed. She *was* young. "Vietnam. Two tours. I'm fifty-eight."

"Oh. Wow."

"Yeah."

He said he had liked going to hear jazz in New Orleans. One night he'd taken a woman to hear the Dukes of Dixieland, and she'd asked them to play some old standard, and they wouldn't play it. He'd felt bad for her, because she was so disappointed.

"What song was it?"

Catch shrugged, not wanting to admit he remembered. "Some old song they used to play a lot. I don't remember the name."

"I just had to get out of there," Nancy said, shaking her head as if she could still hear the wind.

"You could've picked a better vacation destination," he said.

"Y'all got it better here. At least you have the sand and the sunshine. New Orleans is trashed worse than New Year's Eve, and *no one's* coming to clean up. It stinks."

"It can get to a person."

They were silent for a while. Catch had not talked like this in a long time, and he had not been with a woman for even longer. Cleaning up at the Zimmers', he'd gotten to where he could decide quickly what could and could not be fixed; what was damaged beyond repair and what was salvageable. When he came into town and saw people, he found himself sifting through them the same way.

Catch got up to go to the bathroom and ran into Martin. "Hey, Catch. I forgot to say earlier: I was sorry to hear about Norma."

"Hear what?" Catch said.

Martin dropped his head. "They found her with her husband, Sam, and that baby they were raising. They tried to ride it out in an apartment complex in Gulfport. It wasn't a sturdy place. Not many of those Gulfport complexes made it. But they found their bodies."

"Didn't know she married."

"Sam was a good guy. They took in that baby after a friend of theirs died. I'm sure there'll be services. I'm real sorry," Martin said, putting his hand on Catch's shoulder.

When Catch returned to the table, the waitress laid the bill in front of him and mentioned that karaoke was starting up in the bar.

"They serve booze?" Nancy asked, popping two painkillers. She put two more pills in Catch's hand. He looked at them, then swallowed them with his beer.

"Lemme buy you a drink," Nancy said.

"We're crazy tonight," a drunk woman Catch didn't recognize said to them on their way into the bar. She was pushing tables back to make room for dancing. A construction worker danced alone in his work boots, leaving little piles of dirt on the linoleum. Black ceiling fans whirred, and the muted TV glowed with the evening news. Volunteers, probably from New York City, stood at the bar with their goatees and their weird little eyeglasses. The locals sat around tables crowded with half-gallon bottles of vodka, cans of pineapple juice, and buckets of ice.

"Jesus," Nancy said.

"We know how to party," Catch said, trying to sound game. "Eleven dollars gets you a bottle, a bucket of ice, and a mixer. In New Orleans, for the same price, you can get, what, maybe one drink with a stupid name?"

Catch saw Jed Saucier messing with the karaoke equipment, pressing buttons to make the lights flash. Jed was a high-school dropout and a lousy shrimper, but since the storm he'd bought a karaoke system with lights and was traveling with it from shack to shack up and down the coast. He'd told Catch one drunken night that these sound-and-light machines got him laid and were going to make him a millionaire. Some girls in scuffed high heels were dancing with each other and singing, *Rub it in, rub it in.* Jed made a red laser light squiggle on the ceiling and switched to a new song, something about talking dirty in Spanish.

"People have changed," Catch said, feeling a need to apologize to Nancy.

"You seem OK." Nancy touched his arm; then she touched the bandage on her forehead and looked at her hand.

"You all right?" Catch asked.

"I feel a little dizzy."

He could see a circle of brown-red blood on the bandage.

"Come on," he said. "This is bullshit anyway. You should be lying down."

They rolled down the truck's windows on the drive back toward the Gulf. The air was cool and perfect, and the sun had just finished setting. Catch pointed out a light near the shore, a lone fisherman spearing flounder. The evening was beautiful and calm, the sky already full up with stars the size of prawns. A few boats were harbored at the docks, where some men tonged for oysters. How could it have ever been anything but this? It was hard to imagine all that water coming up so high and so far. Twenty-two dead in Pass Christian, and they were still finding bodies. Norma. He hoped she hadn't suffered.

He turned in at the Zimmers' house and helped Nancy out of the truck.

"Man," she said, looking all around her. "How did this place survive?"

Catch laughed. "*Survive*'s a funny word for it." He had cleaned the house and yard up quite a bit from what it had been. The only time he'd out and out cried was when he'd cut a child's twisted blue nightgown from the crepe myrtle.

The shell of the big house looked eerie and sad in the dark. The roof and outer walls were still there, but everything inside—the mahogany tables, the cypress settees, the marble sideboards, the needle-pointed chairs—had been torn up or washed away altogether. The place wasn't much more than an empty wreck in an empty, ruined town.

"It was the second oldest house in the Pass," he said. "Now it's the oldest."

"It's so sad," Nancy said.

That's what they all said. *Sad*. He thought on that itty-bitty, three-letter word. There had to be a better word for this feeling.

Catch told her about how deep and wide the porch had been, and how the wind and water had ripped the boardwalk from the beach and crashed it into the house like a battering ram.

"From where I was, out back, it sounded like the world was coming to an end."

"That's what I thought too," she said. "Where I was."

He explained how the water had gotten into the sand and undermined the foundation, dooming the house to collapse. "They still have that guest house out back and enough land to build on," he said. "We're just waiting to put a crew together to get started."

"How come you have to wait?"

"The lady. The Missus. Mrs. Zimmer. She just died and then the permits. It's complicated." Together they looked at the house again. "It was a hell of a house," he said, as if he felt a need to defend the wrecked edifice. "I put that roof on myself."

"And it held," she said.

"Yeah, it did. And I'm gonna stay and help them rebuild." He felt as though he had decided this right then, after she'd said, *It held*.

They heard a loud bang, and Nancy jumped toward him, her hands on his chest. Her chin touched his shoulder, and her hair smelled of crayons. He put his arm around her.

"Was that a gunshot?" she asked.

"Probably just somebody's car backfiring."

There was a time when he'd liked a scared woman, had even liked scaring women himself, just so he could play the hero to his own bad guy. It was getting dark.

"You can stay the night," he said. He moved his arm from her shoulders, opened his trailer door, and turned on the lights. The electricity was steady again. She looked at the ground.

"It's good the trees are coming back," she said.

Already a cluster of crepe myrtles were blooming pink, and the banana trees had survived. The pink hydrangeas he'd planted around the back of the house had even started to bloom. The salt water hadn't killed everything like everyone had said it would. Most of the live oaks were green. So many trees had come down, but the Zimmers had lost only one. The trees looked different now, though: more gnarled and twisted.

"I wonder where that dog is now," Nancy said, sounding sleepy.

"Probably long gone." Catch bent to pick up a scrap of paper, this one from what looked to be a children's book: *Then and only then I understood the reason. Her fears had been for my safety. The serpent had bitten me just above the ankle. "Must I die?"* There were bits of yellow and red left of an illustration, and the tail of something, maybe the serpent. He put the paper in his pocket.

"What do you think would've happened to me if you hadn't come along?"

Catch thought he smelled the stench of the dog on his fingers. "Come on."

It was tight quarters inside the trailer. There was the kitchen with its toy-sized plastic sink, a table with two attached seats, and then the bed in back, taking up almost half the space. Spread out on an empty flour sack on the kitchen counter was a sea of broken bits of blue and white china, and next to it a stack of glued-together plates. Catch saw Nancy looking at it.

"Crazy, I know," he said.

"I've seen worse," she said, putting her hand on one of the plates. He wanted to ask her not to touch it, wanted to explain that the stuff was not his. He wanted to tell her that this was how he spent his nights. Each time he passed the counter, he might see how one piece fit into another, and day by day, week by week, he'd glued plates, bowls, cups, and saucers back together, working through four tubes of Krazy glue.

"Do you think they'll ever use them?" she asked.

The dishes all had cracks and chips he could never fill. Sure, this made them more delicate and likely useless, but didn't it also make them more valuable in some way too?

"They belonged to her mama's mama."

Once upon a time, in a U. S. Army hospital in Japan, he had lain next to a man blown apart by shrapnel. An officer had come around their beds and pinned them with Purple Hearts, saying words Catch couldn't remember. Now here he was standing at the counter of his FEMA trailer, Krazy-gluing old china plates back together. The world seemed even more dangerous now than it had back then.

"Doesn't this go here?" Nancy asked, holding up a fragment of a dinner plate with the tail of a pheasant on it.

"You got it." He dotted some glue on the edge of the piece she held. "Go for it."

When she made the fit, when the blue picture in the center of a plate came whole, when the tree was a tree again and the fountain a fountain, and the bird had its tail back—well, that was better than a shot of vodka.

"I think I need to lie down," Nancy said. She slipped off her flip-flops and headed for the bed.

Catch opened all the tiny windows to let in the night air. Then he wet a washcloth with warm water and sat on the bed beside Nancy and held the cloth to her head until the bandage was easy to peel off. He felt her eyes on him as he cleaned the wound and taped on a new bandage. Her face was red-brown from the sun, and he wondered, if he kissed her, what she would taste like, and if she would leave him feeling sun-warmed.

"You want another painkiller?" she asked.

He did, but he shook his head. "You might need them later."

Catch heard the crunch of car tires on gravel and shells, and he stood up and saw the lights of a truck pulling up. He took a crowbar from his closet and opened the trailer door wide. "Who's there?" he said. His voice sounded strange to him. He wished he had his gun, wished it hadn't washed away with everything else.

"It's just me." Getting out of the truck was the man who had been painting the neighbor's gate that morning. He stood in the half circle of light from the door, holding a flashlight and a brown paper bag. "Name is Ed. I brought you some peas I grown. Lady peas."

Catch looked inside the bag; sure enough, it was full of newly picked green peas.

"Sorry I didn't shell them for you," Ed said.

"This is awfully nice," Catch said. It wasn't like him to say this. It was something an old woman would have said.

Ed smiled, showing his crooked teeth. "I seen what you done on the beach today. I want to show you something." He walked back to his truck and motioned for Catch to follow.

Inside the bed of Ed's pickup was something black and wet as a seal: the dog, stilled now from a bullet wound in the chest, right about where Catch had kicked it. All muscle and bone, the dog was as impressive dead as alive.

"I followed him after you left with the girl," Ed said. "It took a while, but I got him."

The dead dog's fur was crusted with salt and smelled of ocean. It seemed more fish than dog now. Catch put his hand on the dog's body, near where it had been shot. He could feel the ribs and see its pink tongue hanging out.

"No place for dogs here," Catch said.

"You got that right," Ed said. He climbed into his truck and slammed the door. "I'm headed for the dump."

Catch thanked him for the peas and watched him back out of the drive, the truck pitching at every pothole, the dog's body thumping in the back.

Inside the trailer Catch put the bag of peas in the pint-sized refrigerator, then went to check on Nancy, who was asleep. He thought about waking her to tell her about the dog, but it was hardly happy news.

Catch reached under the bed and pulled out a shoebox. He emptied his pockets into the box, which was full of paper scraps. He thought of the words *critical mass* and all the words on scraps of pages he'd found, the sentences he'd saved, some of which stood out like warning signs or prophesies: *Ordinarily the mean of a population is unknown . . . . When it was full, the fishermen pulled it up on the shore . . . . "Must I die?" . . . The kingdom of heaven is like treasure hidden in a field . . . . This is how it will be at the end of the age. The angels will come and separate the wicked from the righteous and throw them into the fiery furnace, where there will be weeping and gnashing of teeth . . . . To turn the light on, slide the switch forward.*

Maybe someday it would all make sense.

He supposed killing the dog had been the right thing to do, but he was glad someone else had done it.

There had to come a time when all this mess would be over. This was America, for Christ's sake. Things got done. Maybe he and this man named Ed could get together and start their own crew, get to rebuilding. Maybe he and Ed could make that time come sooner.

Catch sat down on the edge of the bed next to the sleeping girl. She stirred, and the tattoo of the sun on her arm peeked out from beneath a blue cotton blanket he'd gotten from a pile Goodwill had set out at a service station after the storm. There wasn't much that belonged to him outright anymore.

"Somebody stole my gal," Catch sang quietly, slower than the old jazz song was meant to be sung. "Somebody stole my pal. Somebody came and took her away. She didn't even say she was leaving." He hummed the next few lines of the tune the Dukes of Dixieland had never played for his new young bride, Norma, on their first night together in New Orleans. He thought of the way she used to be, the way it all used to be, and he kept humming, because he couldn't remember the words.

THE MAN WHO
PAINTED FENCES

He was there helping with the new sewer line because Katrina messed up everything. He started digging using a backhoe. It was an un-secure hole, fourteen feet down. He did this kind of thing all the time. You get confident, and too sure sometimes. That's when you take chances. He was alone. It started to rain.

He was that man on Scenic, the one who painted fences. We always saw him out there, every morning, before the hurricane took away all the houses, even after, where there were a few fences left.

He knew better than to go down that hole by himself. It was raining hard then. The backhoe was still running when we got there, but he was nowhere in sight. Everybody came out of the house calling for him. His wife didn't know what else to do. She was beside herself. She brought out the little boy.

Find daddy, she said to the boy.

Daddy? Daddy? he called. The boy was three, almost four years old. *I saw him near that scary hole*, he said, pointing.

We're hoping the weight of all that dirt knocked him out. The dirt caved in on him from the rains. It makes it hard to breathe just thinking about it, like you can't catch your breath. They had to dig and dig—almost three or four feet down just to get to his head at 7:30 that night. And all along the news people just kept edging closer and closer to that hole. The scary hole. Just like the boy said.

They showed too much on the news. They reported the cause of death before they'd even gotten the body to the coroner's. We know news needs reporting, but sometimes they should show more respect.

It's hardest on her. The little boy is just mad. We tell him, *your daddy's gone to live with Jesus.* He says, *No.* He says, *I want him back here to live with us.*

He was still standing upright, holding his shovel.

ELEVATION

P aul sat at the desk in his study watching the old man walk back and forth on the broken sidewalk in front of the house for nearly an hour before he went down to see about him. It was June and it seemed like everybody was just waiting for BP oil to come to shore. Paul swatted a horsefly from his face as he crossed the front yard.

"Can I help you with something?" Paul said in a voice that was not unfriendly.

"I thought you left," the old man said. Paul recognized him now. Ned Brown, a retired realtor who sold him the house nearly 30 years ago. He lived several blocks away—or used to, anyways, before Katrina. Ned had a fine two-story Creole-style house with a wide gallery on the second floor that overlooked the Gulf. Paul remembered that Ned's house was remarkable in that there was nothing at all left of it after Katrina hit. The entire home and everything in it had been washed away. Paul had not seen him in years. Ned had been a bigger, darker-haired man back then, the sort who threw noisy bonfire parties on the beach every Fourth of July. Now he looked frail, and, Paul thought, confused.

"I did leave, for a while. Stayed with my daughter up in Chicago," Paul said, taking Ned's hand to shake it. "But I came back. I see you survived."

"I hated Houston," Ned said.

"That's where you and Carol went? During the storm?"

"I guess so." Ned said. "Lost weight, my hair, maybe a little of my mind too. Hell, I *am* lost. I've got old timers."

"You mean Alzheimer's?" Paul said. "You're not lost. You're right here, in the Pass."

"I don't know," Ned said. "It's a damn mess."

Paul took Ned by the arm and led him up to the porch. He sat him down in one of the rocking chairs.

"Wait here, Ned. Let me get you an iced tea."

Paul went inside, passing through the newly decorated living room, painted with colors his daughter Diane called "Sea Salt" and "Windswept Shores." Diane and her son Teddy, who was fourteen now, had moved in with him after he'd fallen a second time and shattered his left elbow this past winter. Paul poured the iced tea, then got out the phone book to look up Ned's address so he could tell him where he lived.

"You're way up in DeLisle now," Paul said, carrying the drinks out onto the porch. "Safe from hurricanes *and* oil spills."

"She couldn't stop crying. She couldn't eat. We couldn't, you know, find anything, not a damn thing," Ned shrugged. "And then, I just lost her."

Paul thought for a minute. "You mean your wife, Carol?"

"After the divorce I came back here. Couldn't stay away." Ned laughed. "You know I'm from Kansas? Well I'll tell you what. I'll tell you what. What's your name?"

Paul thought briefly about how awful it must have been for Ned in Houston, how cruel his wife must have been to divorce him after all they'd been through together. She must be a terrible person.

"Paul Zimmer," Paul said. "You sold me this house back in '85."

Ned looked down at the ground for a moment. Paul waited. "Ned?"

"I may not be able to recollect numbers or streets. And sometimes I forget to eat, but I remember my wife."

"I'm sorry to hear about the divorce, Ned," Paul said. "That Katrina did a number on all of us."

Ned looked at Paul, seeming to consider what he'd just said. Then he stood up and went to the edge of the porch and looked out toward the beach. He pointed toward a boy who was digging around in the sand.

"He one of yours?" Ned asked, nodding toward the boy on the beach.

"Grandson," Paul said. "Teddy. You met him a few times when he came down to visit."

The boy was chin-high, his delicate shoulders browning in the sun. He was out there on the beach looking for oil balls. Teddy had a rough time of it at his new school this past spring—his sharp Chicago accent probably made it worse. When she was alive, Paul's wife, Mary, had lavished Teddy with attention, especially when they visited their daughter and Teddy in Chicago, even taking violin lessons with the boy. After the hurricane, when they moved in with Diane and Teddy, Mary was able to put all her energy into Teddy. But Paul could not. He spent his days in his daughter's big apartment watching cable news shows reporting on the hurricane's aftermath and seething over the bad deal he was offered from the insurance company. Mary took care of the boy, their only grandson. Then Mary died. A year later Paul came back to the Gulf alone to rebuild their home.

"We had a grandson, you know," Ned said looking out toward the Gulf. "He's somewhere."

"Do you mean, you lost your grandson? In the storm?"

Ned shrugged. "I don't think so. I don't know. Your lawn needs cutting."

"Our man, Catch," Paul said. "He's gone. Not enough work for him around here, I guess." Catch up and left town with a New Orleans woman, and Paul had not heard from him since. Catch's leaving felt like a last betrayal.

It was sunny and hot. Paul and Ned watched Teddy kneel down near a black figure lying on the beach. Why hadn't Paul seen the figure before?

"Don't touch it!" Paul yelled. It was most likely covered in oil, though there was still no oil in sight. Was it a dead body? It most certainly was something animal.

"DeLisle you say?" Ned said. "That really where I am now? That's where everything landed after the storm. Me and the debris."

When Teddy knelt to touch whatever it was on the beach, Paul shouted to him, "Teddy, no! Get away from there!"

The three of them stood around the beached dolphin, their shadows falling over the animal. It looked to be young, its skin scarred and bleeding. Both its eyes were shut, swelled to the size of oysters, but its blowhole looked clear, and it was alive, breathing in short spasms. Their presence didn't seem to move the dolphin one way or the other.

"Leave it be," Paul said.

"We *can't* just leave him be," Teddy said. "He'll die."

"It can't see," Ned said. "Even if we got it back out to deeper water, he'll just get lost again. He looks like a gonner."

"Ned's right, Teddy."

The dolphin was a gonner, Paul thought, and wasn't this exactly the kind of survival-of-the-fittest life lesson that would be good for a boy like Teddy? *Animal Planet* up close.

"I think we should save it," Teddy said.

Neither man had a cell phone. Paul looked up and down the beach hoping maybe someone else could take charge. Up toward town, he could see some men putting up the Ferris wheel for the seafood festival in front of the Catholic church, even though the fishermen weren't allowed to fish. Paul looked back up toward his house, rebuilt after Katrina.

It looked big and sturdy from where they stood. The contractor jacked it up a good many feet and poured concrete pilings there, there, and there. Katrina had shoved his house right off its foundation but Paul moved it back into place, bolted it down, and there it sat tucked into the live oaks, its wide galleries on all sides.

So much had gone into the rebuilding. For two years, he and Catch, the yard man, would listen and chuckle at the town's same old complaints about how the rebuilt houses might not be "in keeping" with "historic aesthetics." How could there be any aesthetics without houses or people? "Screw 'em," Catch would say. "Paint it polka-dot if you want."

"What is it, again?" Ned mumbled, staring down at the dying mammal.

Teddy looked at Ned. "It's a dolphin."

Ned shrugged his shoulders and shook his head.

"You alright there, Ned?"

Ned looked over at Paul, saying nothing.

"Grandpa. Can't we do *something*?" Teddy asked.

The police gave Paul the number of a marine mammal research center in Gulfport. While Paul called, Ned and Teddy stayed down on the beach, in the shallow waves, keeping the near-dead dolphin company.

A rescue crew came, young guys in their twenties wearing flip-flops and sunglasses, their leader a dark haired, dark-eyed woman named Daphine. She seemed half-dolphin herself, getting down in there, kneeling in the water with the injured dolphin, whom she said was a "he."

"You don't think this is a BP dolphin, do you?" Paul asked.

"I don't see any oil on him. We're seeing a lot of animals swimming away from the plumes, but all those oil dispersants could have gotten to him," Daphine said. "Who knows? Nothing's normal out here anymore."

Daphine left a message about the dolphin on a BP hotline. A lady from the local newspaper came down to the beach and took pictures. There were so few locals left, Paul wondered who was even reading the local newspapers. The lady reporter interviewed Teddy who spoke quietly but clearly. "He seemed to come out of nowhere," Teddy said. "And he looks pretty bad. I hope he'll be all right."

Daphine and her crew managed to lift the sick dolphin into a small pool of water in a pickup truck to transport him to their facility in Gulfport.

"Come and visit as often as you want," Daphine said.

Paul offered to drive Ned home, and on the way back from dropping him off at a barren apartment complex in DeLisle, Teddy insisted on stopping at the little bookstore out there in a temporary structure. He wanted to get a book about dolphins.

At the bookstore the back wall was still entirely devoted to books about Katrina. The bookstore manager handed Teddy a book about Gulf Coast dolphins. The manager was wearing green and purple Mardi Gras beads even though it was summer. He pointed to one of the hurricane books on the wall display with a sign that said *Katrina 50% off*. "That one has a CD with opera music so you can cry while you look at the pictures. My best seller." He wasn't smiling. He shook his head. "This hurricane has gone on too long."

That night after dinner, Teddy cleared the plates while he told his mother about the beached dolphin. Diane was going at the new granite countertops with a special sponge. Paul could tell she wasn't listening. Lately, Paul would find himself watching his only child, now a divorced, middle-aged woman, move about his house with a strange sense of detachment, like she was some kind of benign intruder. A temporary guest. They had never been close, he and Diane, hadn't even lived in the same state for nearly 20 years, and now that she was living with him, the tension between them was compressed, more palpable, and Paul began to accept the fact that he didn't like his daughter very much.

Before Diane and Teddy moved in, Paul had hired a woman named Alice to help out after his first fall. Alice was forty-three years old and she complained of female problems, back pain, and a stubbed toe. She told Paul she didn't really like being a caretaker, but she was having money troubles, just like everybody else around who had lost everything in the storm.

Paul pitied the woman, much more than she pitied him. This was when there were still endless disputes over insurance and nothing was getting done, and some lawyer up in Oxford got hauled away for bribing a judge and pocketing embarrassing sums while FEMA families were still living in FEMA trailers.

Every day for two months this woman named Alice woke up in Paul's home, ate food out of his refrigerator while filling out some sex quiz in a woman's magazine, left dirty dishes in the sink, then parked herself on his new sofa in front of his new flat-screen TV and turned on the Movie Channel. She had to sit, she said, because of her toe.

After he fell a second time while getting his mail, Paul took to writing suicide notes, addressing them, but never mailing them. He wrote the notes at the desk in his study with his arm in a sling, buzzing from a mid-afternoon Scotch, while Alice watched her movies. And for months, all he could think of was how lonely and miserable he was and how plain stupid he'd been to rebuild this house in this God-forsaken place, without Mary, his wife.

Then out of the clear blue, Diane said she wanted to leave Chicago and move to Mississippi with Teddy. For good, she said. Could she move in with Paul? Teddy could attend the private school in Bay St. Louis, and together they could look after Paul. Paul agreed and she managed to sell her condo even in the lousy Chicago real estate market, and when they came down right around Christmas, she decided to redecorate Paul's restored home. Paul gave his new flat-screen TV to the woman named Alice when he fired her. After Diane and Teddy moved in, Paul felt less sorry for himself. He stopped drinking in the afternoons and he quit writing the suicide notes.

Diane's hair had grown out and fell down around her face and to her shoulders in a shaggy, attractive mass. Her skin had taken on an earthy glow because she spent part of every morning walking out in the sun. She had quit wearing makeup or jewelry and she wore soft workout clothes everywhere, as though at any moment she might stop and roll into a pretzel shape the way yoga people did.

Paul stared out the kitchen window. Volunteer trumpet vines bloomed and all the trees that had survived the hurricane were tilted away from the water like women fleeing. He thought about Ned Brown then, and how terrible it must feel to spend every few moments starting over. But then again, there was a lot that Paul would like to forget.

Diane and Teddy loaded the dishwasher. Teddy was still going on about the dolphin and Diane still wasn't really listening.

Lately, Diane had taken to spending entire days in New Orleans picking out knick-knacks and fabric for curtains even though Mary had never bothered with curtains here. She had liked all the light.

"I'm not sure what kind of flowers we want for the House and Garden Walk," Diane said.

"Get roses," Teddy said. "The kind you give a girlfriend." Teddy had a clipboard with a pencil on a string, and he went through the pantry, checking off items on his clipboard.

"What girlfriend?" Paul asked, then winked at Teddy. Teddy was looking through the kitchen drawers and cabinets, checking and re-checking their supply of canned provisions—batteries, flashlights, food, and bottled water. Paul wondered which was worse—the BP oil coming to shore or another hurricane.

Diane went on about the flowers yet to be arranged and the dining room chairs that hadn't arrived, this with only so many more UPS days left before the event. She had multiple lists going on the backs of envelopes all over the house. The Pass Christian Garden Club had asked that Paul's house be included on the House and Garden Walk, and in about a week, people from up and down the coast would be coming through the house, admiring the renovation job and the newly restored gardens. It was pathetic really, having any kind of "house walk" with only about six rebuilt houses total in the town. Paul was not looking forward to the event.

While Teddy went through the pantry, Diane told Paul this was a huge opportunity, maybe the start of a whole new career for her.

"Who doesn't need a decorator right now, when everyone's rebuilding?" she said, hanging a new purchase over the fireplace: an old gas sign that read *Good Gulf* as though she were willing the Gulf waters to be good.

"Not everybody's rebuilding," Paul said. "And the ones who are don't always have money leftover for a decorator."

This decorating obsession was beginning to annoy Paul— she wrote checks from his checkbook without asking and there was never any discussion of a budget. If she liked something, she bought it, then presented it to Paul as if it were a gift to him or something she had made herself. But Paul hoped that by re-inventing herself as a decorator, she might find a good-looking local man, someone with a house to settle down with, so he generally kept quiet about the whole thing.

"Hey, why didn't anyone open this?" Teddy said, holding up an unopened envelope.

"Whoa," Paul said, recognizing the envelope. It was one of Paul's suicide notes, addressed to Diane. How had that gotten away from him? Paul walked over to Teddy and took the envelope, but in one swift movement Diane took the envelope from Paul.

"That's my shopping list," she said.

"I think that's mine," Paul said. He snatched it from her. "It says onions, carrots and celery. You can remember that."

Diane and Paul stared at each other. Paul folded the envelope and stuffed it into his pants pocket. What had he written to Diane anyway? That he loved her? That he couldn't be happy? That he was sorry?

"What are you going to do after all this is over?" Paul said.

"What do you mean what am I going to do? I'm going to continue taking care of you. That's why we came. For you."

Already, he regretted saying anything." All I mean is, you can relax now, right? The house is done. Let's just live in it now."

"Yeah, OK," she said. "The house is done. Your house."

"It's your house too, Diane."

"No. This will always be your house," she said. "Always. And I'm glad you like it." She picked her purse up off the counter and began digging for her car keys. "I'm going to pick up the what . . . tomatoes, carrots, and lettuce. See you later." And she left.

Paul looked at Teddy who was standing by the pantry door, watching his mother walk across the backyard to her car.

"Not sure what happened there, exactly," Paul said.

"Don't worry," Teddy said. "She always gets like this before a party."

Later that night Paul and Teddy sat on the porch, staring out at the open water, waiting for Diane. Paul remembered the time back in Chicago, soon after they moved in with Diane, when she went out to have dinner with the man she was dating. Teddy was maybe eleven years old. Diane called the next morning from the airport, saying that she was going to Montreal with the man and would Paul and Mary look after Teddy until she came back. That's the way Paul remembered it. Paul was furious, but Mary just took it as a chance to spend more time with her grandson. This was the whimsical way Diane lived her life and Mary was used to it. Paul was not. She had taken off the same way twice in college too, and even that one other time in high school. When Diane finally came home, Mary was gone and he never asked Diane how she could just up and leave her son like that.

"You don't tell jokes anymore?" Paul asked. It had been at least two years since he'd heard one of Teddy's knock-knock jokes.

The boy thought. "What do you get from a pampered cow?"

"I don't know, what?"

"Spoiled milk."

"Ha," Paul said. "Another bad one!"

Paul wondered if Teddy ever wondered why he'd come back, but the boy never asked. Maybe because he knew it was a crazy thing to do to rebuild here, right on the Gulf, in the same place after Katrina. And wasn't that diesel he smelled in the night air?

"I guess it could happen again, huh?" Teddy said. They both looked out at the water. A dog barked. Paul wasn't sure if Teddy meant another hurricane or his mother leaving.

The following morning, Teddy sat with Paul in the waiting room at his doctor's office. Diane was at yoga class. She'd come home after midnight, then left the house early that morning with a new to-do list for the House Walk. Other people in the waiting room sat quietly turning the pages of their books and magazines. Paul wondered what illnesses or concerns they all had and why they were there. There was a great deal of cancer in these parts. Breast cancer, pancreatic cancer, prostate cancer, cancer of the uterus, the cervix, the skin. Name a body part and there was a cancer to attack it.

Every so often the doctor would find something to remove from Paul—a questionable mole, nasal polyps, a growing freckle. There was much to do over his prostate, too, and there was always his too-high blood pressure to manage, his poor balance, and his aging heart.

When Paul was healthy the thought of dying did not terrify him at all. But when he was sick—when he was dizzy or throwing up, when he was out of breath and he thought he was having a heart attack, or when he was down on the ground after a fall, that was when he did not want to die. He thought it would have been the other way around.

A receptionist came out with a remote control and turned on the TV hanging from the ceiling. The morning show hosts were sipping beer and wine from Australia. They gossiped about celebrity relationships. People put down their books and magazines and stared up at the TV.

The local news came on then. The governor said there was nothing to worry about, no oil was coming onto Mississippi beaches. Then there on the TV was Teddy's beached dolphin, still blind, but swimming in an inflatable pool. The lady newscaster told the story about Teddy finding the dolphin and they showed a picture of Teddy on the beach, the picture the local newspaper reporter snapped. The TV station announced they were running a naming contest too. They flashed a phone number you could call across the screen.

"Hey," Paul said. "That's my grandson here."

Everyone in the waiting room looked at Teddy and clapped. Teddy straightened in his chair and even smiled.

They stopped for lunch at a little place in Gulfport where they ordered root beers and fried oyster po' boys.

"Eat up," Paul said. "These may be your last." He told Teddy he didn't have to see his doctor for another two months.

"Two months?" Teddy said. "Why not a year?"

"Because when you get to be my age, you see doctors more often. Quit worrying."

From where Paul and Teddy sat outside with their po' boys, they could see Ship Island. Way back, a great-grandfather of Paul's floated on a log from Ship Island to Gulfport, washed ashore from Fort Massachusetts, like debris. Paul wondered if Ship Island was going to take the hit from the oil. After Katrina, Gulfport was a muddier town but more substantial, more meaningful because it bore the weight of a Cat 5 hurricane. The *U Loot We Shoot* signs were all gone, but there was that gradual discovery of destruction that continued to bring sightseers from all over. People got out of cars to take pictures of giant heaps of rubble. Five years after the storm, and there were still torn bed sheets hanging in the live oaks.

"So what *should* we name the dolphin?" Teddy asked.

Paul spotted a black dog, obviously abandoned, across the street. It was covered with scabs and it was slinking around, sniffing for a house to go under. The look in that dog's eyes said, *Shoot me, just please shoot me and get me out of this misery*.

"How 'bout Bubba?" Paul said.

"Mister Bubba," Teddy laughed. Then he thought for a minute, and got out a pen and a slip of paper to begin a list of names. *Mr. Bubba, Flip, Dolphy, Slippy, Tuna, Fred.*

§

They drove back home the long way, so they could see the water. Paul once read somewhere that meditation and water were forever wedded. He figured there was some truth to that. Water could wash us all away, cleanse the soul, bring salvation, clear the mind of rot. Take your pick. Every book Paul had ever owned was somewhere at the bottom of the Gulf of Mexico. Where did everything go? Did it all sink in the sand? Would the oil cover it all like chocolate sauce?

"Water, water, water," Paul said.

"The gulf is so still today," Teddy commented. "You could walk on it."

"Someone tried that once," Paul said. "Caused a big stir."

Driving east on the highway, heading back, he and Teddy both saw the Ferris wheel spinning slowly in front of the abandoned Catholic church up ahead, its lights all different colored against the blue sky.

As soon as they got out of the car, a girl Teddy's age smiled and waved, stopping her bike to tell Teddy what a wonderful thing he had done, saving that dolphin's life.

"Thanks," Teddy said, his face shining with sweat. "I'm still working on a name." Two dimples emerged near his cheeks as he grinned. He had the same alignment of freckles across his nose as Diane had when she was that age.

"High school's going to be a whole lot easier for you next year," Paul told Teddy as they watched the girl leave on her bike.

Clouds hovered over Cat Island and they rose together above the town and above the slate-gray Gulf. The beach went on for miles straight, flat, and white. Inland, out past the people eating cotton candy, funnel cakes, past the families at picnic tables with cardboard boxes full of boiled crawfish, there were miles and miles of longleaf pines. No oil yet. From up here, it really was a paradise. Maybe next time, because there would always be a next time, next time when those waters rose up again in walls, forcing itself into the homes and lives of all those people, maybe next time it will not carry so much away.

Early on the morning of the House Walk, Paul and Teddy helped Diane set up what she called her devastation photos on easels throughout the house. Paul couldn't stand to look at the pictures she had taken of their shattered home right after Katrina. There were photos of all that hand-hewn lumber brought up from Louisiana on schooners before the Civil War strewn about like pick-up sticks; there was his wife's beautiful chandelier mangled and shattered on the back lawn; there was their living room, its floor caved in. The pictures were personal and obscene.

"You sure this is a good idea?" Paul said.

"It's a before-and-after thing," Teddy said. "Compare and contrast."

Diane didn't say anything. She clacked around in heels, adding flowers to arrangements, puffing up pillows, propping them with the corners up like in the magazines. It had rained the night before and the air smelled fresh and tinted with jasmine. The hawthorns were putting out new leaves and the crepe myrtles were blooming. The bar stools had arrived and the pine needle mulch spread all around the flowerbeds. The curtains were late because the curtain lady was having a baby, but Diane hung them up anyway late the night before. She had even put vanilla bean in the ventilator to make the house smell wonderful.

Guests were already arriving. "This is what it looked like right after the storm," Diane said, directing their attention to the appropriate, awful photo, then waving a hand toward the room in which they stood. "And this is the same room now."

Paul joked with himself about putting up his own historic markers throughout the house. Here is where Mary and I laughed, played, and made love. Here is where we became a couple again. He walked around as though seeing the place for the first time. The rooms were immaculate, but it wasn't all neat and tidy so as to forget the violence done it. She re-hung the bent chandelier from the dining room mostly as they had found it, but with new shades. And all around, there were other signs of the house's struggle. Paul saw pieces of his wife's china displayed here and there on the restored fireplace mantle, on side tables, and inside an armoire, plates and saucers that belonged to her mother and her mother's mother, which Catch had glued back together. In the library, on his bookshelves, broken bits of an urn, the rusted iron alligator, a ruined fork, a bent, square-headed nail, reminders, all.

Paul didn't particularly want to talk to any of these strangers, mingling around him in his living room. Most of them were survivors come to walk through other houses to see how other people were managing. He thought of their homes all over the coast, their walls stained with watermarks, showing how high the water went and when it backed down. He thought how he and all of them were stained now, and how everyone on the coast was connected pel-mel by mud and water.

Paul saw Ned come though the front door and walk into the living room, wringing his hands. Ned went straight for Diane, who was in the middle of telling a small crowd around her how lucky they had been, lucky enough to rebuild. She pointed to a nearby picture of a rubble heap.

"It was still a home, even when it was beaten down and on its knees," she said. "It's amazing just how much you can salvage from a life, isn't it? Once you raise yourself to higher ground." Some people sighed. One woman leaned into Paul and said how proud he must be to have a daughter like Diane.

"I thought you left," Ned said to Diane, wringing his hands. Paul could tell by the far-away look in Ned's eyes that he was confused again.

"I just moved here recently," Diane said. "This is my father's house."

"The people may all be changing," Ned said. "That much is true. But there will be a tomorrow because of this water water water."

"Excuse me?" Diane said. "Do I know you?"

"Ned!" Paul said, hooking his arm around Ned's. "It's me, Paul."

"Do you know this man?" Diane whispered to Paul. "Could you please get him out of here?"

"Let's go get some air, Ned." Paul steered Ned away from Diane and away from the crowd.

"You don't belong here," Ned shouted, then leaned into Paul. "She doesn't belong here."

As soon as Ned sat down in a rocking chair, he stared up at Paul. "I'm sorry—do I know you?"

"Yes," Paul said. "I'm Paul Zimmer. You sold me this house."

Ned nodded.

Paul took a deep breath and looked out onto the Gulf where he saw Teddy walking on the beach. He smelled the dark, distinct odor of oil.

Paul turned to Ned. "I've got an idea."

Daphine met them with a bucket of fish. Ned applauded when he saw the dolphin swimming in an elevated blow-up pool. Daphine showed Teddy how to feed him fish from the side of the pool. She speculated that the dolphin was probably a year or two old and had probably been separated from its mother in a storm. They'd done blood tests and discovered he had a gastro-intestinal infection in addition to a urinary tract and an eye infection. They'd given him antibiotics and nursed him back to health.

"You've done a lot," Paul told Daphine. "I guess I'd lost hope in the poor guy."

"He won't be able to swim in the wild because now he's too tame," Daphine said. "Sharks would get him. But you fix what you can. And he *is* alive."

She was a revelation, Paul thought, this girl with the pretty face and thick legs. She was a mix of Mexican and Mississippian and who knew what else, and she was magnificent. The dolphin swam through hula-hoops, around boogie boards, buoys, and balls. Teddy and Ned laughed when it swam through the thick green felt strips donated by a nearby car wash.

"You come up with a name for him yet?" Teddy asked.

"Response to our little contest has been pretty weak," Daphine said. "Got any good ones?"

Teddy nodded. "Well, since you say he's probably from Louisiana, how about Cajun?"

Daphine looked at the boy and smiled. "Cajun," she said, smiling at Paul. "I think we have a winner."

Two days after the House Walk, Paul, barefooted, went for a glass of orange juice in the kitchen, and when he came back with the glass of juice, he tripped over the corner of a new rug and fell. He went down hard, hitting his head on the marble floor in the back gallery. He had not seen the chair that had pulled up a corner of the rug. From the floor, Paul stared at the flipped up rug and its rough brown underside.

He couldn't move his hand because he couldn't feel his hand. He couldn't lift his head to look at his hand. He calmed himself by rolling into a more comfortable position on his stomach, and he breathed. He lay there nauseated on the floor, his mouth dry. Teddy was on the beach. Diane said she was going to yoga and then to a meeting in New Orleans. She wasn't sure when she'd be home. Paul had hugged her that morning, then kissed her, telling her how proud he was of her. She didn't say anything then, nor had he commented on the size of her over-stuffed gym bag when she left.

Paul pressed his cheek against the cold floor, which felt almost like the cool washcloths his mother used to fold on top his forehead when he had a fever. In his mind, he checked his heart and any other organs he could think of. He lay there, still, and waited for another thought to come to him.

The Rubáiyát of Omar Khayyám was somewhere out in the Gulf, its pages swollen with sea water, but the verses were still in his head:

There was a Door to which I found no Key:
There was a Veil past which I could not see:

Some little Talk awhile of Me and Thee
There seemed—and then no more of Thee and Me.

Lying there on the cool white marble, Paul wondered if he had any life beyond this moment. And yet, he wasn't afraid. He attempted to think about all the little pleasures he had known such as petting a dog's ears, drinking coffee while reading the paper at breakfast, wearing a fine hat and good-fitting gloves, turning the clock back every fall. He drifted away, wandering the halls of a house that he knew to be his home, but was not his home. He walked through empty rooms and furnished rooms only to arrive at yet another door and another. He opened door after door, with dread and fascination, hoping maybe to find his wife, Mary, sweet Mary, daughter of a wagon maker from Pennsylvania. Her face had been a painting, the brushstrokes changing every year.

He approached a heavy door with an iron-black handle. He tried the door, but something was on the other side and it wouldn't open. He pushed at the door. He leaned in, and with his shoulder, he pushed and pushed.

"Grandfather?"

The light had changed. There were dust motes in the air all around the boy's head. Someone had opened a window, and the delicate curtain lifted in the breeze, bringing in the smell of jasmine. Paul drifted back to sleep, wanting to return to the labyrinth of rooms. He knew that Mary was in there somewhere. If he stayed in the house long enough, he would find her. It was a matter of finding the right room, the right door. He smelled the decay from damp wood. He could hear the gulls outside.

"Grandfather?"

The boy touched Paul's fingers and Paul opened his eyes.

"You're going to be OK," the boy said. "I'm here and you're OK."

The way Paul felt about the boy just then, it felt as though he had lifted himself up and left a part of this country, a disquieting, but not altogether unpleasant sensation. Barefoot like that on the floor, smelling the beach air made Paul think of the Gulf Coast of his youth and the way the air smelled after a summer rain.

Paul could feel the boy's hand in his hand, a hot, sweaty hand.

He was no longer The Married Man or The Working Man or The Family Man or The Widowed Man. He was a boy from Mississippi again, barefooted. The boy came back to him, reconstructed right there on the floor of his reconstructed home. His walls and roof were back up, and this barefooted, sweaty boy came unannounced, his grandson and his younger self, both. He'd come out of this red and sandy southern soil and so he would return.

He could hear the high whining noises of chainsaws in the distance. Why are they sawing trees?

"That's the ambulance, Grandfather. I called for help. They'll be here in a minute."

There was so much he wanted to tell the boy. There was so much.

He heard the crunch of oyster shells and gravel on the driveway, then car doors slamming and the sound of heavy shoes on the gravel.

"That's them," Teddy said. "That's the paramedics."

"How long have I been down?"

"I'm not sure. I was gone for an hour, maybe two. I found oil balls and a dead shark."

He took in where he was and what had happened: the pulled up carpet, the broken juice glass on the back porch, the smell of rain coming up from behind. He saw a note with his name on it in Diane's neat script. It must have fallen from the coffee table as he fell. He did not have to open and read the note to know what it said. She was gone.

For a moment, he thought he might be dead because everything went white, but he was not dead—he was still here. He remembered days that had been, the games he played in the backyard and on country roads growing up, years with his lovely Mary. Why had he come back without her?

This is for you, Paul wanted to say right then to the boy. *I came back for you.*

"Grandfather? Are you OK? They're coming. Just stay still."

Paul cleared his throat. "How did the tree feel after the beaver left?" Paul said. Teddy shook his head. "I don't know. How?"

"Knot so good," Paul said, spelling out *k-n-o-t* until the boy laughed.

ACKNOWLEDGMENTS

Many thanks to the National Endowment for the Arts for awarding me a fellowship to complete this book, and to the Fulbright Commission for sending me to Hungary, where I read many of these stories at various conferences and readings. My thanks must also go to Jim Kissane, M. M. Lieberman, Lynne Sharon Schwartz, Donald "Skip" Hays, Jim Whitehead, Bill Harrison, Heather Ross Miller, and Barry Hannah—teachers, mentors, and friends who have stayed with me in so many ways; Molly Zimmer, Mary and Ray Gallegher, Nita and Ben Beall, Sarah Dabney Gillespie, Alan Huffman, Ann Abadie, Sally James, the Mississippi Library Association, the Mississippi Institute of Arts and Letters, Pass Christian Books and so many others who kept me afloat; Edward FitzGerald, translator of *The Rubáiyát of Omar Khayyám*; Pat O'Connor for being a saint; and to my father, Jim McMullan, who gave so much to so many, always.

CREDITS

The stories in this book first appeared in the following places:

"The Man Who Painted Fences," in *Fiction at Work*, Chicago, IL, Nov. 2, 2009.

"Mont Royal," in *Freight Stories*, Number 5, Summer 2009.

"What I Want To Know Is When Did Barbara McIntosh Get To Be So Jealous?" in *TriQuarterly* issue 132, Northwestern University Press, Evanston, IL, Spring 2009.

"The Aftermath Lounge," in *The Sun*, Chapel Hill, NC, December 2008.

"The Swing," in *The Sun*, Chapel Hill, NC, issue 384, December 2007, and in the anthology, *Christmas Stories from the South's Best Writers*, edited by Charline R. McCord and Judy H. Tucker, forward by Elizabeth Spencer, Pelican Press, Louisiana, fall 2008.

"Hurricane Season," in *The Southern California Anthology*, University of Southern California, Los Angeles, CA, Vol. XVIII, 2002; also in the anthology *Not What I Expected*, edited by Donya Currie Arias and Hildie S. Block, Virginia, Paycock Press, 2007.

"Place Value," in *You Must be This Tall to Ride*, University of Alabama Press, Alabama Spring 2010.

"Insurance," in *Arkansas Review*, Arkansas State University, Arkansas, Fall 2010.

"Elevation," *Louisiana Literature*, Southeastern Louisiana University, LA, Spring 2012.

ABOUT THE AUTHOR

Margaret McMullan is the author of six award-winning novels for adults and young adults including *In My Mother's House, How I Found the Strong, When I Crossed No-Bob* and *Sources of Light*, which was nominated for the National Book Award. Her books have won Parents' Choice awards, honors from the School Library Journal, the American Library Association, and Booklist. Margaret's work has appeared in *The Chicago Tribune, Southern Accents, TriQuarterly, Michigan Quarterly Review, Ploughshares, StorySouth,* and *The Sun* among other journals and anthologies. She received a Fulbright to research and teach at the University of Pécs in Hungary, and she is the National Author Winner of the Eugene and Marilyn Glick Indiana Authors Award.

Margaret currently holds the Melvin Peterson Endowed Chair in Creative Writing and Literature at the University of Evansville in Evansville, Indiana and serves as a Faculty Mentor at the Stony Brook Southampton Low-residency MFA Program. *Every Father's Daughter*, her anthology of essays by women writing about their fathers with an introduction by Phillip Lopate is out in Spring 2015. Margaret received a National Endowment of the Arts Fellowship in literature to complete *Aftermath Lounge*.

Calypso Editions is an artist-run, cooperative press dedicated to publishing quality literary books of poetry and fiction with a global perspective. We believe that literature is essential to building an international community of readers and writers and that, in a world of digital saturation, books can serve as physical artifacts of beauty and wonder.

CALYPSO EDITIONS

INFO@CALYPSOEDITIONS. ORG | WWW. CALYPSOEDITIONS. ORG

Fiction and Nonfiction
CALYPSO EDITIONS
www.CalypsoEditions.org

THE LITTLE TRILOGY
By Anton Chekhov
Translated by Boris Dralyuk
Fiction

HOW MUCH LAND
DOES A MAN NEED
By Leo Tolstoy
Translated by Boris Dralyuk
Fiction

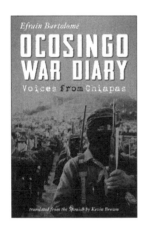

OCOSINGO WAR DIARY:
VOICES FROM CHIAPAS
By Efraín Bartolomé
Translated by Kevin Brown
Nonfiction

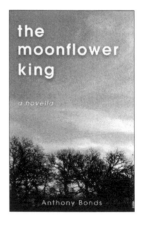

THE MOONFLOWER KING
By Anthony Bonds
Fiction

Contemporary Translation
CALYPSO EDITIONS
www.CalypsoEditions.org

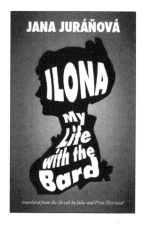

STOMACH OF THE SOUL
By Sylva Fischerová
Tranlated by the author, with
Stuart Friebert and A. J. Hauner
Poetry

ILONA. MY LIFE WITH THE BARD
By Jana Juráňová
Translated by
Julia and Peter Sherwood
Poetry

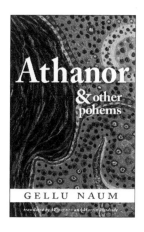

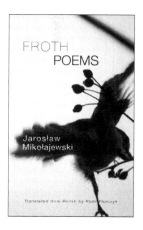

ATHANOR AND OTHER POHEMS
By Gellu Naum
Translated by MARGENTO and
Martin Woodside
Poetry

FROTH: POEMS
By Jarosław Mikołajewski
Translated by Piotr Florczyk
Poetry

Poetry

CALYPSO EDITIONS
www.CalypsoEditions.org

CITY THAT RIPENS
ON THE TREE OF THE
WORLD
By Robin Davidson
Poetry

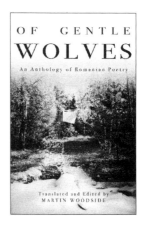

OF GENTLE WOLVES:
AN ANTHOLOGY OF
ROMANIAN POETRY
Translated by Martin Woodside
Poetry

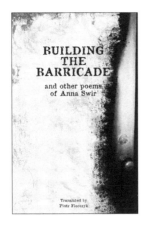

BUILDING THE BARRICADE
AND OTHER POEMS
OF ANNA SWIR
Translated by Piotr Florczyk
Poetry

USE
By Derick Burleson
Poetry